TALISMAN

MJ MUMFORD

TINY BLUE
DRAGONFLY
PRESS

TALISMAN

Cover by
Elizabeth Mackey

ISBN 978-1-7773362-9-5 (ebook)
ISBN 978-1-0691490-0-8 (paperback)

Reading Order & Content Guidance

Talisman opens on the fateful moment when our brilliant, charming, utterly unprepared Dr. Morley Scott stumbles on the power of timeblinking.

This novella can be read at any point in the timeline. Explore it before the main series to get to know this key character, or dive into afterward to discover something about Morley that will probably shock you.

If you have any content concerns, please review the Guidance page at mjmumford.com before reading.

Chapter One

M orley had simply blinked.

In the next disorienting instant, he was stumbling backward, his arms grasping for a dining table that was no longer there and into a void where his chair had stood moments before. He landed on his back with a thud, the impact jarring his teeth and awakening that old football injury at the base of his spine.

For several panicky seconds, his lungs refused to expand, as though the surrounding atmosphere had turned to congealed grease. When he finally sucked in a breath, he was struck by the strange taste of it—citrusy and fresh, yet carrying notes of fried food, new carpet, and...was that *jet fuel?* The smells bore no likeness to the precisely cooled air circulating throughout his Port Raven penthouse.

Morley blinked again, willing his surroundings to shift back to the familiar confines of home. Instead, the scene remained impossibly alien. It was a cavernous space dotted with rows of empty vinyl seating and large, floor-to-ceiling windows looking out into the darkness. There, he could only see the odd tall lamppost casting pools of light onto what looked like an empty parking lot.

Inside, the foreign space was strewn with splashes of harsh, focused light bouncing off polished linoleum floors, reminding him of all the examination rooms he'd worked in the past twenty-odd years. In the distance, a garbled female voice cycled through what sounded like recorded announcements.

An airport. He was in an airport. And he was alone.

Morley's mind reeled, trying to make sense of a nonsensical situation. A vivid dream? A psychotic break? He pinched the skin on the back of his hand. The pain was sharp. Real. Not a dream, he confirmed, though he couldn't rule out psychosis.

Struggling to his feet, the world tilted, and he faltered sideways, catching himself on the arm of a nearby row of seating, the faux leather upholstery cool against his palm.

His gaze darted around the desolate departure lounge, searching for something—anything—to give him an indication of what was happening. He spotted a sign above a raised counter. The letters swirled in and out of focus before snapping into sharp, alarming clarity: SFO Gate 34.

San Francisco? The thought was so absurd that he let out a muffled laugh, disturbing the quiet space. Surely it was a mistake. He was in Port Raven, Washington State, over eight hundred miles north of the hilly Californian city.

He closed his eyes, hoping that when he opened them again, he would be back in his dining room where he'd been moments ago, but when he allowed himself a peek, nothing had changed. His chest tightened, each breath becoming a painful, conscious effort. Sweat gathered along his hairline and down his back despite the air conditioner's chilly flow.

Morley fumbled at his wrist, counting his pulse. The steady thrum beneath his fingertips was fast, but not dangerously so. One-ten at the most.

He patted himself down, a part of him still expecting to find evidence that this was all some elaborate hoax. His clothes felt right—the crisp fabric of his dress shirt, the slight give of his dark gray slacks. His modest, Swiss-made watch remained a reassuring presence around his wrist. He wished he could say the same of his other possessions, but his pockets were empty. No wallet. No keys. No phone.

Morley sank onto a chair and let out a strangled sound, halfway between a laugh and a sob, when he saw his feet. There, incongruous against the airport's industrial carpet, were his favorite slippers—the tan moccasins his Aunt Marion had given him for Christmas two years prior. He'd been wearing them as he sat at his dining room table mere moments ago.

At least I'm fully clothed, he thought, remembering a string of med school anxiety dreams where he'd shown up to exams buck naked. This had to be the same thing. A dream. A very vivid, very bizarre dream. But even as he thought it, he knew it wasn't true. The dim lounge, the distinct smell of jet fuel, the lingering ache where he'd landed on his back—it was all too visceral to be a product of his sleeping mind.

He forced himself to breathe. Panic wouldn't help. He needed to think, to observe. He scanned the lounge again, his doctor's instinct for detail asserting itself despite the surreal circumstances.

He observed a young man he hadn't noticed before tucked into a dark corner, eyes closed, white electronic cords snaking from his ears down to...was that an *iPod* in his hand? Morley shook his head. Surely, he'd been mistaken. He hadn't seen one of those ancient devices in years.

At the far end of the lounge, a janitor pushed a floor polisher in slow circles. The machine's comforting hum and the mundane scent of lemon cleaner created a surreal coun-terpoint to Morley's internal chaos.

Neither person seemed to have noticed Morley's sudden appearance. Small mercies, he supposed, though the thought did little to quell the jumble of questions in his mind. How had he gotten here? Why was he here? And most pressingly—how was he going to get back?

Amidst his roiling thoughts, an unexpected image surfaced: Syd Brixton—his friendly neighborhood bartender who was always eager to discuss her latest TV obsession. What was that speculative fiction show she'd convinced him to watch? *Dark Mirror?* He'd finally relented and started the series, but after a few episodes of tech-driven nightmares and alternate realities gone horribly wrong, he'd abandoned it. Too bleak, he'd told Syd, preferring the relaxed escape of travel and cooking shows.

Now, standing in this impossible airport in his unpressed designer clothes and suede slippers, Morley let out a bitter laugh. If this was the universe's way of telling him he should have stuck with the series—*Black Mirror*, he remembered now—it had one hell of a sense of humor. He promised to forgo his adventures with the late, great Anthony Bourdain when he returned home and give Syd's show another try. That was, if he ever made it home.

The implications of his precarious state crashed around him in waves: no money for food or shelter, no ID to prove his identity, and no way to contact anyone for help. Who would he call, anyway?

With a vague worry that he might have died and been relegated to angel- or ghost status, he made his way to the nearest washrooms and stood in front of a sink. Relief surged through his veins when his own face stared back at him in the mirror, undeniably real, without a hint of translucence or ethereal quality.

"Lucky me. I'm not some sad ghost stuck in an airport for eternity." He snorted a laugh, musing that if he were doomed to haunt such a place, he'd have preferred the Changi Airport in Singapore. The place was a small city of its own.

Morley reached up to adjust his tie—a habit ingrained over years of professional life. But it wasn't there. Instead, his fingers brushed against something else: his silver dragonfly talisman hanging outside his shirt. No bigger than a quarter, the pendant nonetheless commanded attention. Its delicate, feminine design was an unusual accessory for a man, but Morley wore it next to his heart for a reason. It had belonged to his beautiful wife, Collette, before she passed away four years ago. She'd rarely taken it off during all their years together, and when Morley inherited the piece, he vowed to do the same to keep Collette's memory alive.

He tucked it back into his shirt, frowning, once again wondering what had become of his tie. He was certain he'd put one on today—in fact, he knew he had because it was the sky-blue one with white and gray swirls that always reminded him of Van Gogh's *Starry Night*. It had simply vanished during his unexpected journey, alongside his wallet and phone.

Sighing, Morley fumbled with the buttons on his shirt cuffs, finally releasing them and rolling up his sleeves. The soft, expensive fabric now felt like a mockery of his hopeless state. No amount of savings, investments, or his obscenely high credit limit could help him now. He was starting at ground zero.

Leaning over the sink, he splashed water on his face, savoring the shock of the cold rivulets running down his jaw and dampening the collar of his shirt.

"Wake up," he muttered, yanking three paper towels from the dispenser, blotting his collar, and drying his hands. "Come on, man. Get your head on straight. None of this is real." As if to prove it, he slapped himself in the face hard enough to make him cry out in pain. Rubbing the red welt emerging on his cheek, he shook his head despondently. "As if all of this wasn't mind-boggling enough, I've resorted to self-harm now, too."

The sudden sound of a toilet flushing startled him. As he contemplated making a hasty exit, a middle-aged man in similarly rumpled business attire emerged from a stall. A kindred spirit, Morley thought, wondering if the man had traveled eight hundred miles in the blink of an eye like he had. The urge to ask him subsided when the man carefully avoided eye contact, proving he was not a time traveler but just a regular guy doing his best not to engage with the man wearing bedroom slippers, muttering about being a ghost, and slapping himself silly. The fellow gave his hands a brief rinse and departed without drying them, leaving Morley feeling oddly exposed. What worried him more was how quickly his thoughts had ventured to time travel as an explanation for his predicament.

Shaking his head at the absurdity of the idea, Morley refastened his sleeve buttons and steeled himself for whatever lay beyond the door to the departure lounge. He hoped that by some fantastical portal-hopping, time-bending miracle, he would step right back into the comforting sanctuary of his Port Raven condo.

However, when he passed through the door, the stubbornly intact world of the San Francisco International Airport remained exactly as he'd left it.

Beating back panic, he decided he needed to move, to walk, to do something other than spiral into a full-on anxiety attack. Not that he was prone to such things. In fact, his patients' parents often marveled at his ability to stay calm during a child's biggest tantrum.

This time, however, keeping a level head felt nearly impossible. As he set off down the concourse, he reflected on his activities right before he'd been thrust into this bizarre realm, wondering what could've triggered it. Nothing stood out. Everything had been quite normal.

The morning of January 14, 2019, had started like any other in his Pacific Northwest town—cool and unremarkable. He'd been sitting at his dining room table, rifling through an old photo album for a specific picture of his late wife, Collette. The photo in question showed her standing next to the Large

Hadron Collider in Geneva, smiling from ear to ear. His dear Collette, the accomplished quantum physicist who had known all about the mysteries of the universe but not how to beat the ruthless disease that had taken her away from him.

The local TV news station requested the photo last Thursday. They were putting together a week-long feature, spotlighting one local scientist each day. Collette had made the list because of her involvement with the Large Hadron Collider's first operational run back in 2008. Morley had planned to deliver the photo on his way into the clinic, but here he was in San Francisco instead.

He stopped in his tracks. Could the photo of LHC be connected to this unexpected detour?

No sooner had he entertained the idea than he pushed it out of his mind. "Impossible. A photograph can't teleport a person miles away," he said, resuming his aimless walk.

After a few minutes, he stopped at one of several flight status boards distributed throughout Terminal 1. The time indicated it was thirteen minutes past midnight. Morley chewed at his bottom lip, knowing that in the world he'd left behind—wherever that was now—it was a few minutes after six in the morning. He stole a glance at his watch, its second hand ticking along, oblivious, it seemed, to Morley's new setting. The time showed 6:20.

As he continued his restless walk, a vague memory about the San Francisco Airport came to him: fountains. He was sure he'd seen several scattered throughout the terminal, and they'd been littered with tossed coins. A potential source of cash that he knew would eventually be critical if he could muster the courage to wade in and fish them out. Hadn't he seen one in the Baggage Claim area, near the currency exchange kiosk? Or was that a completely different airport altogether? It hardly mattered. The image of a respected pediatrician scrabbling for loose change in a public fountain was too humiliating to contemplate.

No, better to wait until the airport got busier so he could ask strangers for a handout. Surely, someone would take pity on a man down on his luck. The thought made him shudder with shame, but desperation has a funny way of overruling pride. With no credit card to fund his journey back home—or hell, even to buy a simple cup of coffee—gaining access to good old-fashioned cash was his only hope.

So, he'd decided. He would find a comfortable spot to sit and wait for the airport to fill up, relying upon the kindness of strangers to help out a tall, reasonably handsome, fit-looking forty-eight-year-old man with a sprinkle of gray at his temples. He would flash a sheepish, dimpled smile and tell them he'd lost his wallet, then point to his moccasins and explain that his luggage had been mistakenly sent to Tokyo, and wouldn't you know it, his dress shoes had been packed in it. He would further win their pity by telling them he was due at his father's funeral in a few hours and needed proper dress shoes and a suit jacket.

There. He had a plan.

Morley always functioned better with a well-thought-out strategy in place.

He sank into a chair with a view of the tarmac, picking up a discarded celebrity gossip magazine that someone had left behind. Flipping through the pages, he scanned the content distractedly. Something about the Jonas Brothers' purity rings. An article dissecting the latest "Brangelina" drama. A spread on the Beijing Olympics featuring Michael Phelps' record-breaking medal haul. The reference to the Olympics raised the hairs on the back of his neck. Those Games occurred, what? Ten years ago?

Morley closed the magazine and eyed the date on the cover. Indeed, it showed August 2008. He chuckled to himself, thinking, *evidently, the doctor's office isn't the only place to read a stale magazine.*

He tossed the publication aside.

. . .

A moment later, Morley jolted to attention, his neck cracking audibly. He blinked, surprised to find that he'd fallen asleep, and then realizing with dismay that he hadn't been dreaming. He was still in the airport, the sky over the tarmac still dark. A nearby flight status board glowed accusingly: 5:03 a.m. Had he truly slept for over four hours? Or was it another crazy trick of time? Whatever it had been, the number of flights listed on the board had more than doubled, and the lounge had come to life with travelers rushing about.

His stomach growled, reminding him that in his timeline, he'd only enjoyed half a cup of coffee before the universe had yanked him into this strange realm, and the thought of how he might acquire a meal, or even a granola bar, brought his situation back into focus. He needed cash.

Begrudgingly, he made his way towards the Baggage Claim area, each step feeling like an assault on his pride and sense of self. The thought of begging for money made him nauseous, but what choice did he have? Setting his dignity aside, he caught the attention of a kind-faced older gentleman pushing a cart of expensive luggage toward the exit, his wife keeping pace next to him.

"Excuse me," Morley began, hating the desperation in his voice. "I've lost my wallet. Could you spare anything?"

The man ignored him and carried on, but the woman barely hesitated in fetching her wallet from her purse and handing him a twenty-dollar bill. He didn't even have to bring up the lie about his father's funeral.

"It happens to the best of us, dear. I hope you find your wallet."

"Me too. You can't imagine what an inconvenience it is."

Over the next hour, Morley repeated his plea countless times. Some ignored him. Others offered sympathetic smiles and loose change. A few were more generous. By the time he'd circled the area twice, he'd amassed 172 US dollars and a small collection of unusable foreign currencies. It was a lot more than he'd hoped for, but it still wasn't much, considering he had no idea how long he would be stuck in the fine city of San Francisco.

Chapter Two

As some of San Francisco's most iconic structures rolled by the grimy bus window—the Golden Gate Bridge, the Transamerica Pyramid, Lombard Street—Morley allowed himself moments of nostalgia. He and Collette had visited the city often in their younger years, usually for a quick weekend getaway to catch Morley's favorite baseball team in action or to attend one of Collette's scientific conventions. He recalled that right before this surprise trip, one of the photos he'd come across showed the two of them making funny faces for the camera in the stands at a Giants game.

A thought about that photo tickled his brain, but before he could dissect it further, his gaze settled on a modest storefront with a sign reading *St. Martin Foundation Clothing Donation Center*. Perfect. It was exactly what he'd been keeping his eye out for along his journey.

He reached for the stop request button, hesitating for a moment before committing, his pride crowding his thoughts once again. But certain things were necessary if he wanted proper footwear. The bus lurched to a halt, and he stepped onto the bustling sidewalk.

Inside St. Martin's, a familiar musty odor hit him. It wasn't unpleasant; it stirred memories of his grandmother and the church bazaars she'd dragged him to as a child, causing a bittersweet tightness in his stomach.

He perused racks of donated shoes, acutely aware of the contrast between his expensive dress shirt and the worn footwear before him. A volunteer smiled at him encouragingly, and he managed a weak nod in return.

After almost giving up, Morley found a pair of serviceable loafers in his size that didn't look out of place when he tried them on. Next, he rummaged through a bin of new socks and selected a black pair with a blue crocodile logo on the cuff. He took his treasures to the till and counted out a few dollars in change, which the clerk gratefully accepted.

"May I ask you to dispose of these?" he asked, holding up his slippers after he'd put on his new socks and shoes.

The clerk took them from him and turned them over a couple of times in her hands. "Are you sure? They've still got some good life in them. Great quality."

Perhaps the slippers weren't as beat up as he'd imagined and would be a welcome comfort to someone less fortunate.

"Thanks, but I don't need them. Feel free to put them on the shelf."

"I certainly will. If you change your mind, you can always check back to see if they're still here."

Morley smiled and pushed through the doors, thankful for the mild temperature outside. If he had to guess, he would've pegged it at around sixty-five degrees—a far cry from the frosty January morning he'd left behind in Port Raven.

After testing out his secondhand shoes for three city blocks, Morley spotted a flickering neon sign of an internet café. Perfect. He'd been hoping for a library, but this would be just as useful.

The smell of cheap coffee and the click-clacking of keyboards welcomed him inside the café. After paying the clerk in cash and settling into a chair at a monitor, he frowned at the clunky, outdated interface before him. He would've expected an establishment that boasted "Always the newest technology!" and "Fastest internet in the Bay Area!" on its window would live up to its promise.

Feeling vaguely ripped off as the Google homepage loaded (so slow!) Morley noticed the date in the bottom right corner of the screen: August 28, 2008. Cycling his thoughts back to the magazine he'd found at the airport, the outdated clothing, and the older technology he'd been encountering all day, the truth finally hit. His earlier quip had been right. He'd traveled back in time. But that would be impossible…right?

"Holy shit," he muttered, surprising himself with the profanity.

Shaking his head incredulously, he scrolled through the news headlines, each one glaring proof of his displacement in time. Obama's campaign in full swing. The Beijing Olympics dominating sports coverage. And everywhere, ominous rumblings of a looming financial crisis.

Morley's fingers froze over the keyboard as a thought struck him. The photo of Collette in Geneva. The Large Hadron Collider. The date. 2008. He searched "Large Hadron Collider inaugural run" and clicked the first result.

He let out a disappointed breath as he read. The LHC hadn't even started operating yet. According to CERN's latest press release, technical delays had pushed the first test run to September. The photo showing Collette beaming next to the massive particle accelerator wouldn't be snapped for another two weeks.

He sat back in his chair, deflated. So much for that theory. Whatever had catapulted him back to 2008 probably wasn't connected to Collette's work with the LHC at all.

And on the tail of that realization came another one.

Collette.

If this truly were 2008, Collette would still be alive! His heart fluttered as he imagined seeing her again, holding her.

His hand moved to his chest where, beneath his shirt, Collette's talisman hung near his heart. He recalled her smile, her laugh, her striking amber eyes that changed with her mood, and he realized how often he'd reached for her talisman over the past four years—how a simple disc of forged metal could bring him so much comfort. In fact, he thought he might have been holding the piece while he perused those old photos of Collette, moments before some unseen force zapped him to San Francisco.

This made him wonder: Could the *talisman* be the mechanism of the time travel?

He shook his head. The idea was ridiculous, just like his fleeting notion that the Large Hadron Collider photo had anything to do with it. This had to be something else entirely, though he feared he would never learn what that *something else* was.

He returned to the astonishing fact that Collette was alive *right now*. He could get on a bus and go to her this very minute. He would be more assertive, convincing her to open up about the illness she'd insisted on battling alone. With that kind of foreknowledge, he could urge her to seek medical attention earlier. His heart soared. Perhaps that was the whole reason he'd been granted this power. To give Collette a second chance.

But as quickly as the thought came, he pushed it away. What were the consequences of interfering with the past? No, he shouldn't be hasty—not with the limited information he had to go on—no matter how much his heart ached to do so.

Sighing, Morley turned his attention back to the screen. If he was ever going to find his way back to his own time, he would need to educate himself.

Or…

Maybe someone else could educate *him*.

Why didn't he think of it sooner?

He remembered Collette's former colleague, Dr. Burt

Freson, whom Collette worked with at Berkeley from 2001 to 2004 on a groundbreaking project exploring quantum entanglement and its potential applications in quantum computing. Morley had been in Freson's company a handful of times over the years, both at Berkeley functions and once at a dinner party Freson himself hosted. The occasions had been memorable, but not in a good way. Freson was extremely socially awkward and tended to blurt out whatever was on his mind, having little regard for others' feelings. The scientist's childlike confidence had landed him in hot water more than once during the time Collette worked with him.

Quirks aside, Freson was renowned in the world of physics, and if anyone could help Morley with his predicament, it would be him.

Chapter Three

An hour later, a friendly young woman in business attire rapped hesitantly on a door displaying a gold nameplate with "Dr. Burt W. Freson, Professor of Quantum Physics" in black lettering. After a gruff, muffled voice said, "Yes, come in," the woman swung the door open for Morley, revealing a cluttered office filled with bookshelves and whiteboards covered in complex equations.

Dr. Freson looked up from his desk, the prominent bald spot on his head making him look perhaps fifty, but Morley knew he was at least a decade younger than that. Freson pushed his glasses up his nose, his bushy brows raising in what looked like vague recognition. In this timeline, Morley had been in his thirties, so he wouldn't be surprised if Freson didn't recognize his mature forty-eight-year-old face. The scientist didn't stand up to greet him. That was Freson's way. He also didn't offer his hand to Morley. That was Freson's way, too.

"Well, well. It *is* you, Dr. Scott."

"So, you remember me, then."

"Who could forget the kiddie doctor who lured my most

competent colleague away to that godforsaken hippie mecca of the world?”

Ah, it seemed Freson was on his best behavior today. “Not a fan of Washington State, I take it?”

“God, no. I actually enjoy seeing the sun once in a while.”

“Touché,” Morley said. “I was worried you might not remember me, but you and I crossed paths a few times in the past when I tagged along with Collette. You also hosted us for dinner at your Russian Hill townhouse. It’s good to see you again.”

“Yes, yes. Of course. How’s my favorite quantum physicist doing anyway?”

“Collette? Oh, she...she’s fine.” It wasn’t necessarily a lie in this timeline, where she was alive and well.

“A shame she moved to that little hole-in-the-ground lab in Port Raven when she had so much potential here. But I guess that’s the price of falling for the charms of a small-town pedi-atrician.”

Morley didn’t know whether to be offended by Freson’s comment or flattered that he regarded Collette so highly. He chose to ignore him.

“I’m here because I need your expertise on a rather unusual matter. Do you have a few minutes?”

“A very few.”

Freson didn’t offer the chair in front of his desk, but Morley sat on it anyway.

“I’d like to ask you some questions about...*time*. Specifi-cally, the nature of its flexibility.”

“That’s quite a departure from pediatrics,” Freson said, resting his elbows on his desk and clasping his fingers together. “Couldn’t you simply ask your wife?”

The question caught Morley off guard. “Oh, Collette. Well, she,” he stammered before landing on the right words. “She’s extremely busy with her latest project. I didn’t want to distract her, especially when she’s on the verge of a breakthrough. I'm sure you know how she gets when she's in the zone."

"That I do."

Morley's shoulders relaxed. He was grateful the scientist didn't press him for details of Collette's "breakthrough" or why he'd traveled to San Francisco to ask him these questions.

"Get on with it, then. I still have to prepare for my next lecture."

"I was hoping you could bring me up to speed on current theories."

Freson leaned back, the creases between his brows betraying his skepticism. "You mean the current theories on time? That's a broad topic, Dr. Scott. Is there any particular area you're curious about?"

"Yes. I've been wondering about the possibility of human movement through time. Not just forward, but in other directions."

Freson's eyes narrowed. "If I didn't know better, I'd say you were asking me about time travel. And if so, that's the realm of science fiction, Dr. Scott, not physics."

Morley gave the scientist a dejected smile. "Is it, though? Collette bounced her theories off me all the time. She knew the idea of time travel was far-fetched, of course, but she was forever fantasizing about what the world would be like if people could manipulate time and space."

Freson looked at Morley sideways. "You're speaking about her in the past tense. Are you sure she's okay?"

Morley scolded himself internally for the mistake. He would have to be more careful.

"She's fine."

"So, I could give her a call right now?"

Morley's jaw tensed. The last thing he needed was this guy contacting Collette and telling her he was there. If he had indeed traveled through time to 2008, wouldn't his younger self be seeing patients in his Port Raven clinic right now?

Freson shrugged casually, waiting for Morley to answer his question.

"I would prefer you didn't. She doesn't know I've come to see you."

"Well, this gets more interesting by the minute."

Morley stayed silent, unsure how to respond.

"You appear out of the blue," Freson said, "asking pointed questions about quantum theory, while referring to Dr. Scott in the past tense. You must admit, it's a little peculiar."

Like you? Morley thought. "You're right. My being here *is* odd. As I said, I would've asked Collette about these things myself, but she's been busy."

All his life, Morley had gotten along well with most people, but Freson was the exception. The scientist's lack of social skills had been a point of friction between him and Collette the few times they'd all been together. Collette had always laughed off Freson's biting remarks, saying his computer-like brain had only one function: to unravel complex scientific problems—not to engage in the tedium of small talk. Morley, on the other hand, had always contended that even toddlers could learn basic manners.

"Fair enough. I've got seven minutes. What do you need to know?"

Feeling the mugginess of the small office, Morley unbuttoned his shirtsleeves and rolled them up. "What if I told you I've experienced a strange phenomenon of finding myself displaced in time?"

Freson picked up a pen and clicked it several times, studying Morley intently.

Feeling the need to fill the silence, Morley continued. "I know this will sound impossible. Crazy even. But today, for me, it's 2019, and I have no idea how to return to it."

Freson's expression cycled through disbelief, confusion, and, finally, amusement. He tossed his pen onto the desk and barked out a laugh, making Morley jump. "Okay, I get what this is."

"I beg your pardon?"

"Collette put you up to this, didn't she?"

"No, I—"

"Come on. You almost had me there. Time travel? You seriously expect me, one of the top physicists in the country, to believe such an outlandish story?"

"I assure you, this is no put-on."

Freson leaned back in his creaky swivel chair and laced his fingers behind his head. "Surely your lovely wife told you we had this thing going on when we worked together—trying to one-up each other with the most outrageous prank. I'd been the reigning champion when she packed up and flew North."

"That's not what—"

"Ah, that last one was a masterpiece," Freson said, staring glassy-eyed at a spot just past Morley's shoulder. "I reprogrammed her computer to display all her data in binary code. It took her two days to figure out how to fix it. She was furious. But also impressed. Said it was the best *worst* gag I'd ever pulled off."

Morley shook his head. "That's not what this is."

The scientist lurched forward and seized the handset of his desk phone, handing it to Morley. "All right, punch in her number."

Morley shrank back, imagining the implications of Collette receiving such a phone call. A call where this annoying former colleague claimed that her loving husband was sitting in front of him this very minute—in San Francisco —spewing nonsense about being a time traveler from eleven years in the future. To which Collette would say, "Nice try, Freson. Morley's at his clinic right now." Morley glanced at his watch, seeing it was 11:35 in 2019. Freson could argue that it was only a two-hour flight, so it was entirely possible that Morley had hopped on a plane this morning instead of going to work, and that Collette would have been none the wiser.

But as Morley thought back to that time, if Collette *had* received a strange call like that, wouldn't she have mentioned it to him? Maybe Freson decided not to call her after all. Morley decided to call his bluff and keyed in her number at the lab.

"At least it will prove I'm telling the truth," he said, handing the phone back to Freson. "Though I figured you'd want to be the first quantum physicist who knew time travel was possible."

Freson raised the phone to his ear, keeping his eyes glued to Morley. "You're full of shit."

After a faint, tinny ring broke the silence, Morley shook his head in mock disappointment, "Just saying. It's your career."

Freson licked his lips, keeping his gaze trained on Morley.

Two more rings. Good. Collette wasn't available.

But after a fourth ring, Morley heard the small, sweet sound of Collette identifying herself in Freson's ear. His heart faltered. God, he would do anything to talk to her, but he knew he couldn't. Not here. Not yet.

Freson licked his lips again, staying quiet.

Collette's thin voice drifted into the silence once more. "I'm away from the office this week and will return on Tuesday, September second. For urgent concerns, please call—"

Freson slammed the phone onto the base. "You'd better not be wasting my time, Dr. Scott. As I said, I'm a busy man."

"I'll get to the point then," Morley said, realizing with amusement that of course Collette was away. She was here, in San Francisco—with a younger version of Morley, probably enjoying lunch at an upscale café on Market Street. "There seems to be no better explanation for what's happened to me than time travel, bizarre as it sounds."

Freson went uncharacteristically quiet as he appeared to mull over Morley's claim. "You mentioned you and Collette having discussions about quantum theory. Did she ever speak about the ongoing search for pentaquarks?"

Morley felt his heart tighten. "Yes," he said, resting his forearms on his thighs and intertwining his fingers. "I believe it was mid to late summer of 2015 when Collette first mentioned it to me."

Freson flashed him a skeptical frown. "Have you always been able to recall the dates and subject matter of your conversations with your wife so well?"

"Just the ones that were extremely important."

"Indeed, the quest for pentaquarks is a hot topic in the scientific community. But why would any of it matter to a pediatrician, to the point that he can remember a conversation that happened four years ago in his natural time?"

Vaguely uneasy that he was about to divulge information that only a time traveler would know, Morley felt he had nothing to lose. "Because she was on her death bed when she told me that pentaquarks were finally discovered."

Freson's face dropped. Morley couldn't be sure if it was because of the news of Collette's death, the discovery of pentaquarks, or both.

When the scientist remained speechless, Morley went on. "Despite her illness, she remained fiercely devoted to the advances in her field right until the end."

"That sounds just like Collette," Freson croaked out, overcome with an emotion Morley still couldn't quite decipher.

"She did her best to explain the discovery to me, and surprisingly, I was able to glean more than a cursory understanding. The details escape me now, but I recall her saying something about the quarks having to be of a certain composition."

"I'm sorry for your loss," Freson said with a sincerity that caught Morley off guard.

"Thank you. It did come as a shock. She was only forty-four."

"Such a shame. Do you remember the composition of the pentaquarks?" he said, abruptly changing the subject back to physics. "Or what types of quarks were involved?"

Morley's mind swam, wondering if a correct answer was the one thing that would get him back to his own timeline. He dug deep into his mental archive, pulling up details he hadn't expected to find. "Believe it or not, I do remember bits and pieces. She mentioned *up quarks* and *down quarks*. And…a *charm quark*, I believe? Yes, that's right. She definitely talked about a charm quark."

"You have a great recollection for details that—as you claim—happened four years ago."

"I don't imagine anyone could forget the term 'charm quark.'"

Freson didn't react. "Did she say anything else? Maybe something about an anti-charm quark?"

"Now that you mention it, yes. I remember joking that it sounded more like a witch's spell than a physics term."

"Fascinating. Did she happen to divulge the particle count for this exotic baryon?"

Morley gave the physicist a bemused look. "I'm afraid that's beyond my limited grasp of physics. Is it important? Will this information help get me back to my own time?"

"Good gracious, no. None of this is relevant to time travel. I was merely looking for proof that you were telling the truth."

Morley's shoulders slumped.

"I'm still not convinced. Collette very well could've primed you to bait me with this so-called discovery of pentaquarks as a desperate attempt to knock me off the prank podium," he said offhandedly, though it sounded to Morley like he was hoping it was all true. "Now, if you could provide credible numbers for the pentaquark states, I might be more inclined to believe your story."

Morley shook his head in frustration. "Look, if this was Collette's elaborate ploy to one-up you, don't you think she would've anticipated your skepticism and given me some plausible-sounding numbers?"

Freson leaned back in his chair, folding his arms across his narrow chest. "Who's president in 2019?"

Morley bit his lip. How he wanted to blow the scientist's mind. "I'd prefer not to say."

"Why?"

"That kind of foreknowledge could potentially influence the course of history, and I sure as heck don't want to be responsible for *that*." Morley snickered. "You'd never believe me anyway. Besides, I could give you *any* name; it doesn't prove a thing."

"So, I have no other choice but to take your story as gospel."

Morley thought of a different tack. "When was the last time we were all together? You, me, and Collette? Three years ago, perhaps?"

"About that, yes. Collette was here for the Particle Dynamics Symposium in '05. I suppose you were there, too."

"I was. A young pup at the time. Take a good look at me. If you honestly think I look thirty-eight right now, then you might want to consider getting new glasses. I'm telling you, I'll be fifty next year."

Freson gave him a long, hard once-over. "I suppose we could always order A DNA methylation test to—"

"Go right ahead," Morley interrupted. He would love nothing better than to see the look on the physicist's face when the results came back, proving he was older than he should be. "But that could take weeks. I'd like to go home *now*."

"Dr. Scott, if what you're saying is true, it would shake the foundations of physics."

"Why do you think I came to you? An esteemed expert in the field?"

Freson brushed off the flattery. "How did it happen? Was there a machine? A specific method?"

Morley pictured the dragonfly talisman under his shirt. He still didn't want to divulge his suspicions about it. "I'm not sure. It happened so quickly. One moment everything was normal, and the next, I was wandering around SFO."

"Did you experience confusion? Restlessness?"

"Sure. Wouldn't you be out of sorts after traveling eight hundred miles and eleven years back in time—in the blink of an eye? It wasn't until late this morning that I'd confirmed the date."

Freson's questions came faster, more urgently. "What else did you experience? Were there any physical anomalies? Visual disturbances? Any sense of rapid movement or feeling like you were floating? How long did the temporal leap take?"

Morley shifted uneasily in his seat, worrying he'd revealed too much. But in the next breath, he said, "There was a physical object involved. I was touching it when the event occurred. I'm wondering if it caused the displacement."

Freson leaned forward, his eyes practically bulging out of his head. "What kind of object? Was it technological? Chemical?"

Morley shook his head. "I'd rather not say. At least not yet."

"That won't do," Freson said, his forehead creasing with frustration. "If we're to understand how it happened, I'll need all the details, or we'll never figure it out."

"So, it sounds like you believe me."

"Let's just say I'm entertaining the possibility. That's what science is all about: keeping an open mind while seeking robust evidence."

Morley rubbed his chin where traces of stubble were already coming in from his early morning shave. "It's personal. And to be honest, I'm not entirely sure of its significance. I don't want to lead you down the wrong path with speculation."

Freson's nostrils flared slightly. "Dr. Scott, if you have truly found a way to defy the natural boundaries of time, every detail could be crucial. Withholding information could hinder our understanding and potentially your chances of…" he cleared his throat as if disbelieving his own words, "…your chances of returning to your own time."

"I understand all of that. But until I'm certain of its role, I'd prefer to keep that aspect to myself."

Freson's lean frame deflated slightly with disappointment. "Very well," he said. "Let's focus on what you *are* willing to share. You mentioned being at home one moment and then at the airport the next. Were there any other changes you noticed immediately?"

Morley nodded, grateful for the shift in focus. "Yes, of course. The time of day had changed. It was early morning when I left 2019, but midnight when I arrived in 2008. And, of course, my location had changed dramatically."

Freson clicked his pen and scribbled the information in a notebook he'd produced from his desk drawer. "And what was the date?"

"January 14, 2019. A Monday. I'd been looking at some photos before going to work."

"These photos. What did they depict?"

As Morley recalled them, he became even more convinced that not only did the talisman have something to do with his journey through time, but so too did the photos. "They were mostly of Collette and me. Several showed us on a trip here, to San Francisco. Another captured Collette standing next to a section of the Large Hadron Collider."

In the ensuing silence, Freson's desk phone buzzed, startling both men. The scientist snatched up the handset and growled into the receiver, "I'm busy."

Morley could hear an indistinct female voice as Freson fluttered his eyes closed in apparent irritation. "Very well. Tell them I'll be there in five minutes."

He slammed the phone down and sprang out of his chair.

"As much as I'd like to delve into this further, I have an extremely full calendar. Can you come back tomorrow at one?"

"Tomorrow?" Morley hoped he'd already be back in 2019 by then.

"It's the best I can do, I'm afraid."

"Yes. Sure. I'll be here."

On his way to the door, Freson grabbed a suit jacket off a shabby couch covered in papers, books, and various items of clothing. Morley followed.

"Can you recommend a budget motel nearby? I was empty-handed on my arrival and had to resort to panhandling to fund my basic needs."

Freson shook his head in amazement. "If this ends up being a big hoax, you'll certainly get the Oscar for most convincing performance, Dr. Scott."

"I'm telling you. I only have the clothes on my back and a handful of donated cash. I bought these shoes at a thrift shop."

Freson glanced at Morley's feet and lifted his bushy brows. "You could've done worse, I suppose. Look, I'd offer you a room at my place, but I have family visiting." He returned to his desk and pulled a key out of the top drawer. "You're welcome to crash on my couch here. It's not the Ritz, but it's comfortable enough. Here's my extra key. I'll alert Campus security so they won't bother you."

Producing his wallet and flipping it open, Freson counted out some bills. "Here's some play money. It should be enough for a few meals. The faculty lounge is just down the hall—they have vending machines and a microwave if you need them. You'll also find restaurants and a grocery store within walking distance of the campus."

"Thank you," Morley said, nearly declining the cash but coming to his senses. He didn't know how much longer he'd be in 2008.

Freson waved off the thanks. "It's the least I can do for my favorite physicist's temporally challenged husband."

The next morning, Morley found himself in a quiet corner of UC Berkeley's library, surrounded by stacks of books and scientific journals. The wall clock showed 11:30. He'd been there since nine, poring over time travel theories and searching for any credible instances of its occurrence. So far, he'd found nothing.

His research had begun the previous night in Freson's office. Unable to get comfortable on the lumpy couch, Morley had managed only about two hours of fitful sleep, having spent the rest of the night perusing Freson's extensive collection of books and papers for information on time theory.

When he was still empty-handed at dawn, he'd ventured out, ducking into Sonnie's Diner, a ten-minute walk from Freson's office in the South Hall. The hot breakfast and strong coffee had done little to revive him; weariness clung to him like a wet blanket.

Now, thankful for his solitude in the grand library, he anxiously anticipated his meeting with Freson in a few short hours. What if the scientist couldn't help him and he was stuck in 2008 permanently? Would he use the predicament to his advantage and find a way to prevent Collette's death in 2015?

Closing the book before him, he drew the talisman out of his shirt, tracing the dragonfly's delicate wings with his thumb. The metal was warm in his grasp as if it held some inner energy. He wondered again if Collette had known about its power, but he dismissed the idea. They never kept secrets from each other. Ever.

He studied the talisman in his fingers, imagining Collette doing the same thing when she had worn it. "So, the question remains, my mysterious little dragonfly: how do I get back to my own time? Are you the key?"

Suspecting once again that he'd been holding the piece at the time of his unexpected journey, he'd tried several things since Freson had left him yesterday: clicking his heels together while clutching the talisman, spinning in a circle three times while wearing it, dangling it like a pendulum and willing himself to be hypnotized. He whispered incantations, tried meditation, and attempted to recreate his exact pose from the moment he'd jumped through time. All of it, futile.

Now, slumped gloomily in his chair in the library, exhausted and out of ideas, he gripped the talisman tighter between his thumb and forefinger and muttered, "Return." And in the next instant—

Chapter Four

Morley thumped onto his dining room chair, disoriented, breathless.

"Oh my god!" he yelled, taking in his surroundings.

Photos and half a cup of coffee sat exactly in the same place as he'd left them.

Joy, relief, and utter exhaustion hit him at the same time, as if he'd just finished running a marathon. He supposed he *had* been on a marathon, searching for a way home. And he *had* made it home, ostensibly by holding the talisman in his hand and reciting the word *return*.

As he gathered his bearings, he discovered two peculiar absences: the wad of cash he'd stashed in his pocket…and his St. Martin's shoes.

Had it all been a dream?

If so, where did his socks come from? He knew he hadn't put any on this morning. Or rather, yesterday morning. Laughing nervously, he pulled up a pant leg, exposing a blue crocodile logo on the sock's cuff.

"Huh," he said, not exactly surprised.

His eyes drifted to his coffee cup again. Was that steam rising from its surface?

Sure enough, when he reached out and felt the cup, it was hot to the touch. He jumped up, sweeping his head left and right, wondering if his housekeeper had entered the apartment in his absence, but after a thorough search, he found he was alone.

He grabbed his phone off the table and gasped when the screen lit up. The date and time showed 6:08 a.m., January 14, 2019.

"Impossible," he said, even though the evidence suggested otherwise. "I can't have only been gone for five minutes."

He ran a trembling hand through his hair and began pacing the room, where everything looked ordinary and intact. His buttercream leather couch. His floor-to-ceiling windows. His sweeping view of the harbor from his eighteenth-floor penthouse suite. The sun peeking over the horizon. All normal. Everything just as he'd left it...thirty-six hours ago.

"I'm a time traveler," he whispered, barely able to convince himself of the fact.

But it was true.

He'd traveled through time.

He sank onto his couch. "It had to have been a dream."

When his gaze fell on the photo albums strewn across the dining room table—the ones he'd been looking at right before he was yanked into 2008—he jumped up and hurried over to them. The photo closest to where he'd been sitting lay face down, Collette's handwritten note staring up at him as if shouting through time: *San Francisco, August 28, 2008.*

He visualized a hundred puzzle pieces swirling in circles, slamming together, and forming a complete picture before his eyes.

He'd uttered that date the moment before he'd jumped a decade into the past—he was sure of it—and he'd been holding Collette's treasured talisman at the time. He was sure of that, too.

His heart twinged with that old familiar ache. He wished Collette were here right now, experiencing this magic alongside him. Because that's what it was, right? Something magical? Or was it pure science—concrete and completely explainable?

His phone pinged with a reminder about an Interdisciplinary Clinic meeting at ten o'clock. He began pacing again, wondering how he would ever be able to focus on work. It was only Monday, and he knew his schedule for the entire week was jam-packed with appointments.

Knowing his mind would be too preoccupied to provide the proper care his patients deserved, Morley fired off a message to the clinic staff on his phone, notifying them that he was taking the day off and likely the remainder of the week as well. He couldn't remember the last time he'd done such a thing. Years ago, probably. Yes, it had been during Collette's last days battling her illness.

He would use the time off to prove that what he'd experienced had been real. That it had not been an incredibly vivid dream or hallucination. And how would he achieve this? By trying it again.

"Am I nuts?" he asked the empty room where only the faint hum of early morning traffic and the whir of the refrigerator reached his ears. "Assuming I can replicate a trip to the past, there's no guarantee I could make my way back again. Was that all there was to it—holding the talisman and saying *return*?"

With his phone still in his hand and the memory of his adventure threatening to escape him like the last threads of a dream, he quickly opened his dictation app, VoxLog, and pressed *Record*. The red button stared back at him, pulsing gently as if urging him to speak, to make sense of the madness that had just unfolded. He slid onto a stool at the kitchen island and brought the phone to his lips.

"Journal entry, January 14, 2019," he began, glancing at the wall-oven clock. "It's 6:17 a.m."

Catching his reflection in the oven door, a ray of sunlight played across the surface of the talisman, making the dragonfly's wings dance with movement. He shivered.

"The following is an account of the incredible events I experienced over the last thirty-six hours," he said, knowing this particular file would be for his ears only. Even he was struggling to believe what had happened. And since he hadn't heard from Freson in the intervening years—the scientist likely chalking it up to a prank after all—Morley was confident the information would remain his secret alone.

"Is there a connection between the talisman and Collette's research?" he mused into the recorder, brushing the thought aside. They had shared everything and built a beautiful life together. She was incapable of hiding something so important. "Yet, what do I even know about this piece? Only that Collette had inherited it from her grandmother in Peru. As far as I know, neither of them had ascribed any significance to the pendant beyond its sentimental value. That's it. That's all I know for certain."

He paused the recorder long enough to pour himself a glass of water and take it to the dining room, where the photos were spread out on the table just as he'd left them. He sat down and resumed his recording. "But here's what I do know…"

After recounting the events in San Francisco, Morley's email pinged. It was Dr. Coulson telling him not to worry about taking some time off and that he and Dr. Franks would be covering his appointments for as long as he needed. He wished him a speedy recovery and hoped whatever he was going through wasn't anything too serious.

"Good. My workaholic ways are paying off."

With the memory of his fantastical trip back in time

swirling in his mind, a word he'd never heard before popped into his thoughts: *timeblink.*

The term had materialized as if by magic, and he knew at once that it perfectly encapsulated the swift, barely detectable nature of his journey through time.

Energized by this small epiphany, Morley clutched the talisman and once again focused on San Francisco, August 28, 2008, willing himself to disappear from his present surroundings. But nothing happened. Each subsequent attempt left him increasingly frustrated and still firmly rooted in 2019.

Over the next few hours, Morley's efforts grew more desperate and creative. He stood in various poses, held the talisman at different angles, and even tried making himself a cup of coffee and recreating his exact position from that morning. When those failed, he found himself eyeing the clock, wondering for a second time whether the time was important. It had been roughly six in the morning when he'd first timeblinked.

"Maybe that's it," he said, setting an alarm on his phone for the next morning.

As the sky darkened and an almost debilitating exhaustion settled in, he glanced wearily at his watch, shocked to discover it was already nine o'clock. He laughed to himself. He'd been so focused on replicating the timeblink that a whole day had passed, and he hadn't even stopped to eat. He ordered some takeout and then opened his VoxLog app once more.

"It's now 9:13 p.m. I'm so tired I can barely think, but I wanted to document the name I've coined for my experience before I forgot it: Timeblinking. Yes. One moment I'm here, the next—" he snapped his fingers, "—I'm somewhere else. In the blink of an eye."

Later, after devouring a Greek salad and pita bread with three souvlaki skewers, Morley collapsed into bed at around eleven o'clock. Sleep eluded him. His thoughts buzzed with spinning timelines and his dear Collette's face, her smile both comforting and haunting.

As he finally drifted into slumber, an unexpected image floated into his mind, startling him awake: Syd, the bartender from The Merryport—the one who'd urged him to watch that strange sci-fi series. Syd, the fair-haired, blue-eyed beauty with her nose piercing and cursive tattoo on the back of her neck that only showed when her hair was up. Syd, whom he'd been visiting at The Merryport every month for the past four years since Collette's passing, and with whom he'd been raising a glass and toasting their mutual losses: Morley's dear Collette and Syd's identical twin, Isla, who'd vanished a few weeks shy of the girls' twelfth birthday.

The ritual had become a source of comfort for Morley, but now it felt like a betrayal of Collette's memory. How could he think of Syd at a time like this, when he'd just experienced something so profound?

Before he could ponder the significance, he succumbed to a restless sleep and dreamed of two shimmering blue dragonflies flittering around each other under the sun's gentle glow.

Chapter Five

The room was still dark when Morley woke. He reached for his phone on the nightstand and checked the time: 5:33. As his mind cleared from the fog of sleep, he was once again surprised to find Syd's face—not Collette's—at the forefront of his thoughts. The realization brought a pang of guilt that he quickly pushed aside. He was allowed to think about other women, for goodness' sake. Collette had been gone four years.

After getting himself ready for the day, he forced himself to eat a piece of toast with peanut butter. Just before six, he slid into his seat at the dining room table with the photos spread out exactly as they had been yesterday morning. The smell of a steaming cup of coffee fueled a renewed optimism.

For the next hour, Morley attempted multiple timeblinks, each leaving him frustrated and firmly stuck in 2019.

Not ready to give up, he decided a change of scenery was in order, especially now that he'd called in sick and could conduct his experiments wherever he pleased—and he had a fine 3200-square-foot log cabin at Sandalwood Lake in which to do so. Out at the lake, away from the constant reminders of his normal life, perhaps he could make sense of the extraordinary events of the past two days. He laughed giddily. "Or should I say, *one* day?"

At ten o'clock, he pulled down the long gravel driveway to his lakeside retreat. Nestled among towering pines and ancient cedar trees, the cabin was his sanctuary, and he could always count on the surrounding air to be fresh and invigorating, no matter the season. January was typically cold, drab, and drizzly on the lake, and today was no exception. It was precisely why Collette had insisted their lake property come furnished with a grand fireplace in the middle of the main floor great room. Morley had been thankful for her doggedness on that front, especially on days like today when winter's bite nipped at his ears.

Despite the cold, Morley decided against building a fire today. If he succeeded in his timeblinking efforts and traveled to another timeline, he couldn't risk leaving the fireplace unattended, even for five minutes. Instead, he cranked up the electric heating and spread the photos across his rustic dining table, just as he had in his apartment. Over the next few hours, he tried every conceivable trick to activate the talisman. All of it in vain.

Frustrated, he grabbed his phone and opened the VoxLog app. "January 15, 2019, 12:45 p.m.," he began, tracing laps around the cabin's expansive living room. "Still no luck replicating the timeblink. I'm beginning to wonder if there are external factors I'm not considering. Could it be tied to a specific location? Or maybe it only works once every... I don't know, lunar cycle?" He sighed heavily. "I sound insane. But I know what I experienced was real."

By one in the afternoon, Morley's head was pounding from the strain of concentration and disappointment. He went to the window overlooking the lake and, seeing that the rain had let up and the clouds were breaking apart, he grabbed his jacket and set off for Chapman Falls, a picturesque national park at the bottom of his road. He needed a good head-clearing walk.

By the time he trudged back up his road ninety minutes later, feeling ready to tackle more experimentation, he noticed a black sedan he didn't recognize idling a short distance from his driveway.

Morley slowed his pace. Who would be up here on a gray Tuesday afternoon in January? Sandalwood Lake only had one year-round resident (Sparkles, the former window washer who'd won millions in the lottery; however, he owned a neon orange Italian supercar, not a nondescript four-door sedan); the rest of the homeowners only vacationed here in the summer. As Morley drew closer to his cabin, he took furtive glances at the mysterious vehicle, mildly bothered by its presence. Maybe the driver was lost? He thought better of approaching car. If the person wanted directions, they would roll down the window and ask.

Morley wasn't given to paranoia, but the sight of the unfamiliar car lurking down the road unsettled him, a feeling amplified by the strangeness of his life lately. Part of him wanted to stay his ground and protect his property, but a bigger part wanted to flee and protect himself.

After packing up his belongings and securing the cabin, he pulled out of his driveway, pretending not to notice the sedan still parked up the road. While he hoped his departure would lure the driver away from his property and his neighbors' vacant homes, the thought of a stranger following him triggered a quiet unease.

As he turned the Range Rover onto the highway leading back to Port Raven, sure enough, the black sedan trailed behind.

"What on Earth are you up to?" he said, ensuring his dashcams, both front and rear, were recording.

Thirty minutes later, as a few fat raindrops splattered on his windshield, Morley turned off the highway, navigating through random Port Raven streets: Dunmore, Oakwood, Smythe. By the time he got to Main Street, the rain had intensified to a heavy shower, and the sedan remained a disquieting presence in his rearview mirror.

He considered driving straight to the police station downtown but decided against it. He was just being paranoid. Perhaps he should stop and confront the driver. Or speed up and try to lose the jerk. The last option gave him a mild thrill, as his vehicle was exponentially faster than the stalker's.

Burdened with indecision, the low-speed chase continued. At each traffic light and stop sign, the sedan inched closer, and Morley found himself holding his breath at intersections, willing the lights to change faster.

As two vehicles progressed, the rain intensified into a deluge, and by the time Morley had circled the city's core twice, water was gushing down his windshield faster than his wipers could clear it.

"This is ridiculous," he said, abandoning his efforts to shake his stalker and pointing his car toward home.

Just as the city began its modest version of rush hour, Morley pulled into the warm, dry parking garage beneath his building. He maneuvered into his assigned spot and wasted no time gathering his things and boarding the elevator to his penthouse.

The ride up seemed interminable as a persistent unease lingered in his belly. That car. Who was the driver, and did they mean Morley harm?

Once inside his apartment, he snatched his navy-blue golf umbrella from the foyer and headed straight for his deck. Extending the canopy overhead, a chill breeze ruffled his hair as he approached the edge, making him shiver. Below, he witnessed a parade of traffic and jostling umbrellas along sidewalks and was glad to be away from both.

He leaned forward slightly, one hand resting on the concrete planter box that served as a railing around his rooftop deck. His eyes scanned the streets, searching for the sedan, but all the cars looked the same under the darkening sky and steady rain.

As he considered going down to the lobby and asking the concierge to alert him of any new, strange visitors that might come asking for him, Morley felt something tickle him at the back of his neck. He realized, too late, that the clasp on the talisman's chain had given way. His fingers fumbled to catch it but missed. All he could do was watch, transfixed, as the talisman and chain plummeted away from him, growing smaller until they vanished from sight.

Morley spun on his heels and bolted through his apartment finding the elevator still on his floor. He dashed inside, punching the Lobby button repeatedly. As the water from his umbrella pooled onto the already-soaked floor, he could have sworn the ride down took twice as long as usual, and by the time the door slid open in the lobby, he was in a flat-out panic.

He burst through the main doors, expanding his umbrella to its full width and joining throngs of people heading home from work, walking dogs, or window shopping.

Maneuvering carefully through the crowd, he scanned the sidewalk, but the wet concrete thwarted him, each crack and glint deceptively mimicking the talisman. He moved east and west along the sidewalk, thinking perhaps the wind had taken it off course and deposited it someplace else, but he couldn't spot it anywhere.

"Hey," came a gravelly female voice from behind him. Morley turned to see a woman whose presence had become part of the street's landscape—a woman who was likely much younger than her appearance suggested. Her face was creased with the harsh lines of street life, her skin leathered by exposure and hardship. Her mismatched, filthy clothes hung loosely on her thin frame, and Morley had to hold his breath against the odor rising from them. In one hand she held a grubby pink unicorn umbrella with two broken tines and a nickel-sized hole in the top. In the other, the talisman dangled in her grasp.

"Are you looking for this?" she said, thrusting it toward him.

"Oh my gosh, yes. It's mine. Thank y——"

"It put a damn hole in my umbrella."

"I'm so sorry. It slipped fr——"

"I was gonna complain to your fancy building management about it, but when I saw ya, I got an idea." Her eyes scanned Morley up and down like he was a member of the Royal Family.

"Oh?" he said, forcing a tight smile.

A dribble of rain seeped through the hole in the woman's umbrella and disappeared into her tangled gray-blonde hair. Unfazed, she jerked her head toward the building. "You do live here, yeah?"

Morley gave the slightest nod.

"Can I borrow a few bucks?"

"I don't have——"

"Like, a couple hundred?"

"I…don't have that kind of cash on me."

"You got a bank card? Don't say no. I know that ain't true."

"I do."

"Well. What d'ya say? You want your necklace?" she asked, swinging it carelessly over a grate in the sidewalk. *She wouldn't.*

"I do, yes. I would very much like it back. It belonged to my late w——"

"Great! Let's go!" the woman said, pocketing the talisman. "I'm sure you know where the nearest bank machine is."

In the shuffle, Morley had forgotten all about the black sedan, but now, as he led the disheveled woman down the street toward the bank, he noticed the menacing vehicle crawling past, holding up traffic behind it. This time, though it was dark, Morley got a look at the driver: a heavyset man with a grizzled salt-and-pepper beard and menacing eyes that bored into Morley's through thick-rimmed glasses. Morley didn't recognize the man, which unsettled him all the more.

For a moment, the busy street and his predicament with the talisman faded away. It was just Morley and this stranger, locked in a silent exchange that crackled with danger.

"Giddyap. I don't have all day," came the woman's raspy voice as the car moved on, disappearing around a corner.

Morley shook his head. Since yesterday morning, his life had spiraled into the absurd: he'd leapt through time, gained a shadowy stalker, and he was about to settle a ransom with a cantankerous street person.

When the transaction was done, he would need a stiff martini. And he knew exactly where to get the best one in town.

Chapter Six

I n the foyer of The Merryport Pub, Morley snapped his new pink unicorn umbrella shut and dropped it into the stand by the door. He groaned bitterly. Between the stalker and the homeless woman's extortion, his nerves were beyond shot.

Heading to his usual spot at Syd's end of the bar, Morley found the pub strangely empty. Of course—it was Tuesday, not his typical Friday when the place hummed with activity. He missed the buffer of that Friday night crowd; tonight he felt painfully exposed.

Shedding his raincoat, he took stock of his unkempt state in the mirrored backsplash behind the bar. The day's bizarre activities had added more creases to his already sloppily ironed shirt, and his hair was sticking up at all angles after hours of anxiously raking his hand through it. Unable to stop himself, he passed his fingers through his hair yet again, finding a small wet patch on the crown of his head. He sighed. Small consolation, he supposed. At least that unfortunate woman would be staying dry tonight under her giant new golf umbrella.

Syd's face brightened when she saw him. "Well, this is a surprise."

"I need a drink." The words came out more tersely than he'd intended, making Syd recoil slightly.

"Everything okay?" she asked.

"Oh. Yeah. Fine." He hung his coat on a hook under the counter and slid onto his stool.

Syd tried to lighten the mood. "I see you have a cute new parasol."

"Ugh," he said, glancing over his shoulder without further explanation. For a moment, he just sat there, staring down, adjusting his leather gloves. He laughed internally at their presence, knowing certain people secretly judged him about the quirk. Fortunately, Syd and the other staff at the pub had accepted that the constant glove-wearing had stemmed from a germ phobia. It was a more plausible explanation than the truth—that he was haunted by the conviction that his touch would bring early death to those he cared about. Collette's demise had been the final straw.

"What brings you to this neck of the woods on a Tuesday night?" Syd asked, wrestling a few strands of long blonde hair back into her bun.

Morley scanned the room, thinking he'd spotted the driver from the sedan sitting at a table in the corner. However, it was just another man with a beard and glasses, and he was much thinner than the stalker. And younger.

"Just needed a change of scenery," he said, bringing his gaze back around to Syd, who was studying him curiously. He flashed her a reassuring smile, but Syd's brows remained pinched with concern.

"The usual?" she asked, reaching for the gin. "Classic martini?"

Morley nodded, noticing he was drumming his fingers on the counter. He forced himself to stop, but Syd continued to eye him uneasily as she fixed his drink. He wished she wouldn't look at him that way, like he was a bomb that might explode any moment.

"Rough day at the office?" she asked, garnishing the cocktail with two olives on a metal pick.

The olives were still settling when Morley picked up the delicate glass and took a long sip. He closed his eyes to savor the welcome burn, and when he opened them again, his thoughts felt clearer, more focused. "Rough day indeed," he said, managing a weary smile.

Syd grabbed a crystal tumbler and filled it with soda water. "Well, it's not our usual night, but how about a toast to Isla and Collette anyway?"

The mention of Collette's name made Morley relax a little. "Guess it can't hurt."

Syd raised her glass. "To your beautiful Collette."

"To your sweet Isla," he replied, trying to maintain his composure despite the panic lurking beneath the surface.

They clinked glasses. Morley drained half his martini in one go, hoping the rush of alcohol would steady his rattled nerves.

"So," Syd ventured. "What happened? Did some kid stuff a bunch of crayons up his nose?"

Morley's chuckle was barely audible over the whine of a blender at the other end of the bar. "Nothing that colorful, thank goodness. What about you? Has the mayor come in to drown her sorrows lately?"

Syd giggled then leaned in conspiratorially. "No, but you wouldn't believe what happened on Saturday. This guy comes in. He's wearing the most outrageous hat I've ever seen. It's a massive sombrero. Neon pink with huge peacock feathers."

Morley raised an eyebrow.

"So, he orders a mojito, and as I'm making it, he hoists a foot onto the counter and pulls his pant leg up. He's wearing a shiny black dress shoe without a sock. Says he's got this pet ferret—"

The mention of shoes shifted Morley's attention to his own issues, the rest of Syd's story fading away. Why didn't his thrift-store shoes return with him to 2019 with him? Was it because they were part of the past and didn't exist in his timeline yet? If so, why did his new socks make it back?

"Earth to Morley," he heard Syd say, pulling him back. He muttered a quick apology.

"As I was saying, this ferret, Screech, is notorious for stealing socks. But only the left ones." She folded her arms and waited for Morley's reaction, speaking again when looked at her blankly. "Well, I thought it was funny."

Morley let out a strained chuckle. "Ah, good one. You made that up."

Syd batted her eyelashes at him. "Whatever do you mean? I swear on The Merryport's liquor collection, it's a true story. Tad can vouch for me."

From the other end of the bar, Tad called out, "Don't drag me into your tall tales, missy!"

Despite himself, Morley smiled, but his mirth quickly faded when he heard the pub's front door open and slam against the doorstop with a bang. He glanced over his shoulder, expecting to see the bearded stranger behind him, intent on settling some old score that Morley knew nothing about. Fortunately, it was just a harmless middle-aged couple who ambled over to a booth near the window.

"Are you meeting someone here?" Syd asked casually. "A date?"

Morley's attention snapped back to her, caught off guard. "I…Yes. I was waiting for someone. But I'm pretty sure I've been stood up."

"Ohhh," Syd remarked with a sympathetic nod. "Well, any woman who ditches you is clearly an idiot."

Syd thrust a hand over her mouth, looking embarrassed, probably thinking she'd overstepped herself. The truth was, Morley didn't mind the compliment at all, especially coming from Syd, whose charm and natural beauty had half the male customers vying for her attention most nights.

Pleased to be enjoying her attention now, Morley said, "That's very kind. Thank you."

Syd took her hand away from her mouth and smiled sheepishly as Morley drained the last of his martini and slid the empty glass toward her. "Another, please."

He noticed Syd hesitate slightly before reaching for the gin. Maybe she was worried he was drinking too much. Or too fast. He had to admit, the alcohol was doing a fine job of dulling his anxiety, so much so that he craved more of that feeling. When Syd set the fresh martini in front of him, he seized it immediately and polished it off in three gulps.

Syd's eyes went wide. "Yikes. Are you sure you're alright?"

Morley waved off her concern. "I'm fine. Just enjoying a little edge remover. And who better to prepare it than the one and only Sydney Brixton," he said, her name coming out 'Shidney'.

"You didn't drive here tonight, did you?"

"Nope."

"You walked?"

"Not a chance. Have you seen the weather out there? I took a taxi."

Syd glanced out the window at the heavy rain. "Can't blame you. Apparently, even the ducks are getting rides."

Ignoring Syd's quip, Morley pulled out his phone. "In fact, I should order a car now."

"There's usually one or two of them hovering around the front door."

"Right. I won't bother calling."

He pocketed his phone and slid off the stool, surprised by his lightheadedness. He swayed a little and had to put his hand on the counter to steady himself.

"Dr. Scott. Are you sure you're okay?"

"Absolutely," he said, digging a wad of crisp new bills out

of his pocket and dropping a couple of them onto the counter. "I'm fine. Honestly. The drinks just hit me a little harder than usual because I haven't eaten yet."

"If you say so."

Morley retrieved his coat from the hook under the bar and shrugged it on. "Thanks, Syd. Talking to you is always a delight. Have a good night."

"You as well. Stay dry."

"I'll try." He stalked over to the door and snatched his tiny pink umbrella out of the stand, holding it up for Syd to see. "How could I go wrong with this stellar piece of equipment to protect me?"

He heard Syd laugh as he stepped into the rainy night, tipsy enough that he'd almost forgotten about his stalker, who wasn't there anyway. He hurried into a taxi waiting at the curb, eager to get home where he could let sleep take him away from this trying day.

Chapter Seven

F our fruitless days of timeblinking attempts had taken their toll, leaving Morley desperate for normalcy.

He leaned back in his chair in his office, the leather creaking as he stretched and yawned. After consuming far too many takeout meals and suffering an embarrassing lapse in personal hygiene, he'd decided to return to the office for the final day of the work week.

The structure of his normal routine had done wonders to take his mind off his failed timeblinking trials as well as the mysterious stalker, who hadn't given up. The guy had been putting in regular appearances whenever Morley left his building, and often enough that Morley had considered reporting him to the police, but the jerk had kept just enough distance that it would be difficult to prove he was a threat.

Now, at the end of Morley's first day back, the pediatric wing had fallen quiet, most of the staff having gone home for the weekend. The covering physicians had caught Morley up to speed earlier in the day, leaving only a few loose ends for him to tie up. He had a good team. They all worked as hard as he did, always putting the children first.

After dictating the last of his clinic notes, his mind

boomeranged back to the talisman and the countless experiments he'd run since Monday. He switched over to his personal journal in the VoxLog app and pressed record.

"January 18, 2019, 6:47 p.m. It's been a crazy week. I have nothing to show for countless hours of timeblinking attempts, having tried everything but turning cartwheels while singing the national anthem."

The mental image made him laugh. "Though at this point, I just might give that a shot." He peered out at the darkened January sky, where a bright white moon peeked through broken clouds. "Surely, I couldn't have imagined the whole thing."

His eyes drifted to a photo in a matte black frame on his desk. He picked it up and smiled. It showed him and Collette at the ballpark in San Francisco on July 10, 2009, a date that would forever be burned into his memory, for it was a day history had been made.

In a completely unexpected turn of events, Jonathan Sanchez—who'd been struggling miserably all season and had been temporarily removed from the starting position—ended up pitching an extraordinary no-hitter against the San Diego Padres, the first for the Giants in thirty-three years.

Morley could still recall the explosion of joy that rocked the stadium when that last pitch sailed over the plate. The city had erupted in celebration, and he'd been there to witness it all, Collette by his side. It was more than just a game; it was a moment of pure magic for baseball fans across the nation.

He pressed the photo to his chest where the talisman hung beneath navy-blue scrubs. "I wish you were here, my darling. You'd probably have this all figured out by now."

Setting the photo down, Morley pulled the talisman out of his shirt, holding it tightly between his fingers. He closed his eyes, funneling all his thoughts toward a specific time and place. A place he'd visited often with Collette.

"Jackson Beach, Friday Harbor, July 16, 1995," he said.

But still, nothing happened.

His eyes sprang open.

"What in Sam Hill am I doing wrong?" he blurted. "Jackson Beach, Friday Harbor, July 16, 1995!"

At once, Morley's chair disappeared, and he toppled to the ground. But it wasn't his office floor he'd landed on. Instead, soft sand cushioned his backside, and the antiseptic smell of his office had been replaced by cool, salty air and campfire smoke. To his left, moonlight danced on dark, lapping water, and in the distance, he could make out a group of people sitting around a crackling fire, their laughter carrying on the gentle night breeze.

"Holy crap!" Morley whispered excitedly, noticing with mild amusement that he'd arrived without shoes. He was, however, wearing socks, which he promptly removed before scrambling to his feet on the shifting sand. He patted the back pocket of his scrubs. No wallet. "Not again," he muttered, knowing categorically it had been there when he'd left. He slipped his socks into the empty pocket and surveyed the scene. He was really here, in the past—at least, that's where he assumed he was. He inhaled a big breath of fresh sea air into his lungs and trudged over to the noisy group around the fire.

As he drew near, their chatter died down. They were young, not even twenty. Two of them eyed him warily, tucking their canned drinks—beer?—behind their backs. One of them, a burly jock type, rose to his feet on the defensive. Morley wondered if the group had mistaken him for a cop until he remembered his scrubs and bare feet.

"Evening," Morley said, trying to sound casual. "Sorry to interrupt, but I'm not from around here, and I've gotten a bit turned around."

The kids stared at him blankly, waiting for him to go on.

"Where am I, exactly?"

The teens exchanged glances at the odd question. A boy

with a mop of shaggy hair spoke up. "Did you, like, break outta Monroe or something?"

Morley chuckled at the kid's assumption he was an escaped convict. "Nothing quite so sinister, I'm afraid. Just a friendly pediatrician who's lost his way. I'm pretty sure this is Jackson Beach, but I just wanted to make sure."

"Yeah, dude. It's JB."

"Awesome sauce." He shook his head at the outdated expression. But then he quickly realized that these kids probably hadn't even heard it yet, here in 1995. Maybe he was the one who'd originally coined the term.

"This next question is going to sound a little odd, but humor me."

The burly kid crossed his arms and grunted.

"What day of the week is it?"

"Duuude, for real?" Moppy-head boy said, clearly the spokesperson of the group.

Morley smiled sheepishly. "I told you it would be an odd question."

"Uh, it's Saturday?"

"And the date…and time?"

One of the girls chimed in. "Are you okay? Do you need to get back to the hospital?"

"I'm fine. Please. Just tell me and I'll get out of your hair."

She glanced at her watch, something kids rarely wore anymore, all but proving it wasn't 2019. "It's July fifteenth," she said. "Well, technically the sixteenth since it's past twelve o'clock."

Midnight again. "And the year?"

Moppy shook his head in disbelief. "What's your deal, dude? It's 1995. Are you a time traveler or something?"

Morley could barely contain his laughter. "Perhaps!"

As he walked away, he heard them scrambling around, packing up. He hadn't meant to scare them, but it was probably for the best. Their parents would be wondering where they were.

Once he was out of sight, Morley paused to take in his surroundings one last time. The gentle lapping of the Salish Sea along the pebbled shore. The crisp night air and the stars twinkling overhead. Not much he could do without a wallet and shoes. Plus, it was the middle of the night. Where would he go?

So, the only choice left was to return to 2019. Once he did that, the miracle of timeblinking would be his to master.

He clutched the talisman like he had at Berkeley and, not necessarily believing it would work, uttered the word "Return."

The world lurched, and at once, he was back in his office chair at St. Bart's. The scent of campfire smoke lingered in his nostrils, and when he leapt out of his chair and sent it twirling off behind him, he noticed a dusting of sand on his bare feet.

"Unbelievable!" He raked both hands through his hair and lodged them there. "How can this be real?"

As he turned and pulled his chair back to the desk, he spotted his wallet on the seat, wondering if the sheer speed of the timeblink had ripped it out of his scrubs. And then, remembering his socks, he shoved his hand into his front pocket only to find it empty. "What crazy mischief is this?"

He sat down heavily, his feet brushing against something firm and bulky under the desk. He laughed when he bent down and found his sensible white sneakers sitting upright, fully laced. He chortled again as he wrestled them back on, wondering why footwear posed such a unique challenge in time travel.

He collected his phone from the desk, delighted to see the VoxLog app still open. *Still recording*. He replayed it back three times, paying particular attention to the timestamps. There was no doubt: he'd been gone exactly four minutes and forty-four seconds from the moment he'd recited his destination until his subsequent return. To think, while he'd spent fifteen minutes on Jackson Beach in 1995, only four and a half minutes had passed in his present.

He pressed the record button. "January 18, 2019, 7:13 p.m.. My audio journal has provided proof of my incredible journey through time. It seems all that's required is to state my destination and date out loud while holding the talisman between my fingers. Hmm. I repeated the command twice. Could that be the key?"

The success of his trip left his mind buzzing with possibilities. He paused the app and stood up. Could he travel to the future?

He went to the window, his eyes glazing over as the city lights blurred into a hypnotic bokeh. What if he timeblinked to 2119, a full century into the future? Visions of what lay ahead flooded his thoughts. Medical breakthroughs. Space travel. Technologies beyond his wildest dreams. What would Port Raven be like? Would it even exist?

He raised the talisman and kissed it, thinking Collette would've given anything for a glimpse of humanity's future. "I wish you were here to witness this with me."

Gripping the talisman, he imagined sleek buildings rising from the ground, flying cars zipping overhead, and holographic displays coming to life in front of him.

"That's all very well and good, but what if the future isn't the utopia I'm imagining it to be?" What if he landed in the middle of a war? Or in a world ravaged by the effects of climate change?

Encouraged by the knowledge that had the power to return to 2019 if he didn't like what he saw, he recited a destination and date exactly a hundred years in the future, repeating it twice.

He licked his lips and waited for the disorienting shift, the split-second blink that would catapult him to a completely different timeline. But nothing happened. His surroundings went unchanged, almost mocking his attempt.

He picked up his phone and unpaused his dictation app. "I've just attempted a timeblink to the future, which was unsuccessful. For now, I'll have to assume that one can only move backward in time, not forward."

For his next attempt, he focused on 1950s New York, where classic cars and smoke-filled jazz clubs promised an authentic glimpse of the city in its prime. After three tries, though, he remained rooted in his Port Raven office.

"It couldn't have been an anomaly. I traveled to the past twice—once to 2008 and once to 1995. But what if," he mused into his phone, "what if 1950 is too far back?"

Confident that was the key, he pictured his majestic log cabin at Sandalwood Lake and the long, birch-lined driveway leading to the covered front porch. He could almost hear the creaky wooden dock and the gentle flitter of dragonfly wings over the water and the way the sun warmed the deck on even the coolest winter day. He gathered the talisman in his grasp. Growing tired of showing up at his destinations in the middle of the night, he wondered if a bit of specificity might help.

"Sandalwood Lake, 819 Chapman Road, nine o'clock, April 26, 2010."

The world went dark for a millisecond before Morley found himself standing on the road at the end of the cabin's driveway. It was the day he and Collette had taken possession of their brand-new property, and they'd been bubbling with excitement to meet with their builder, James, for the final walkthrough.

The handover had been scheduled for ten a.m., a detail Morley would never forget. An hour before that, he'd received a frantic call from his Aunt Marion saying that his Uncle Chuck had keeled over and died of a massive heart attack. And because Morley was Marion's only relative in the city, it meant Collette would cross the threshold of their new dream home without him.

Morley had chosen to revisit that date not only because he wanted to see the joy on Collette's face as she opened the door for the first time but also because he knew that once James was gone, Collette would be alone. With no one else around—younger Morley included—he would have Collette's full attention when he told her his shocking news: that he was a time traveler and that her talisman had made it possible. It wouldn't be too hard to convince her. She would see the lines on his face and the silvery wisps of hair above his ears and know he was telling the truth.

He walked unhurriedly up the long driveway, breathing in the crisp, earthy air, recognizing the subtle scent of lilac blooms wafting on the breeze. He couldn't pinpoint which neighbor's property the smell was coming from; the dense wooded areas on either side of the lot obscured nearby houses from view, creating the illusion of perfect solitude. As he neared the cabin's façade, he had to laugh, recalling Collette's stubborn insistence that this was the back of the house, not the front. She'd maintained that the side facing the lake should be referred to as the front. Morley had found himself constantly confused by which side she was talking about, so they'd settled on a compromise: *roadside* and *lakeside*.

Standing on the roadside of the house now, he closed his eyes and let the familiar sounds wash over him. On other days, he might have heard the roar of Chapman Falls down the hill or the gush of the Deerleg Creek that fed into it, but today, Morley heard only the cheerful twitter of unseen birds in the surrounding treetops.

Mindful that James and Collette would be arriving soon, Morley concealed himself behind a tall Western juniper under a canopy of ponderosa pines and Douglas fir trees.

While he waited, he vibrated with anticipation at the thought of seeing Collette alive again. To gaze into her amber eyes, to smell the light spray of perfume beneath her ear—to talk to her again—what a precious gift.

Most of all, he was looking forward to their discussion about the talisman and its extraordinary power. He would tell her about his unexpected trip to San Francisco and his visit with Dr. Freson. They would share a laugh over the scientist's stubborn skepticism—his certainty that Collette had orchestrated an elaborate hoax for revenge. But beneath it all lay a single burning question deep in Morley's mind: had Collette known about the power all along?

One thing was for sure. He *would not* tell her about the illness that was about to invade her body, and how, in five short years, she would drift free of this earth. That was a conversation for a different time, a time when he was certain he could use his newfound power to save her.

After about twenty minutes, Morley heard a vehicle pull into the driveway, but it didn't sound like Collette's clunky old convertible Rabbit. It was probably James.

Sure enough, a silver SUV coasted down the driveway and came to a stop in front of the house. James hopped out and opened the SUV's back door, fussing with something inside, and when he turned around, he had a young child in his arms. Right. Collette had been annoyed about that. She'd thought it was unprofessional for James to bring his daughter along to the walkthrough, and although Morley had nodded along when she told him, he hadn't really seen the harm.

James set his daughter on the porch and told to her to stay put. The girl, perhaps about eighteen months old, was remarkably obedient. She sat down and babbled incoherently to the knitted mermaid doll in her grasp while her dad unlocked the cabin's front door and swung it wide. Whistling cheerfully, James hurried back to his vehicle and retrieved a massive bouquet of white lilies, transporting it into the house.

The little girl continued playing on the steps while her dad got things ready inside. As Morley shifted to get a better view of the activities, a twig snapped underfoot. The girl's head swiveled in Morley's direction, spotting him before he had a chance to get out of sight. He gave her a little wave, hoping she wouldn't break into tears at the sight of a strange man skulking in the bushes. Fortunately, she waved back and held up her doll to show him her treasure.

Morley ducked back behind the tree when he heard James's voice.

"Who are you talking to, Pumpkin?"

The girl giggled and spewed a bunch of gibberish that Morley didn't understand.

"You saw Uncle Danny?" James asked.

More toddler babble.

"Don't be silly, sweetie. Uncle Danny is at home. In California."

Satisfied with her dad's answer, the little girl stayed silent, much to Morley's relief. He didn't want to explain his presence to James—or why he appeared to have aged nine years in the span of a week. The purpose of this timeblink was solely to reunite with Collette.

Finally, the distinctive cough and sputter of Collette's Rabbit announced her arrival. The antiquated but immaculately maintained car was one more thing he loved about his wife—her nostalgic connection to her first and only vehicle.

Morley braced himself as the white convertible rounded the corner at the top of the driveway, roof down despite the morning chill. Four years of longing crystallized into this single moment—Collette, alive, perfect, untouched by her looming destiny. Her raven hair caught the breeze as she guided the car up the driveway, her signature designer sunglasses making her look every bit the movie star. Morley pressed his palm against his chest, trying to contain the ache of seeing her again on this ordinary Monday that had meant so much to them both.

Collette climbed out of the car wearing a black down

vest over a delicate cream-colored V-neck sweater, her long legs sheathed in her favorite jeans—the form-fitting indigo pair that hugged her curves just right. She removed her sunglasses and settled them on top of her head, eyes sparkling as she admired the architectural wonder in front of her.

Morley forgot to breathe for a moment. "Morley Christopher Scott," he whispered, "you lucky son of a gun."

As he called on every ounce of his willpower not to run to her, his attention went to the little girl, who began spewing a jumble of words in toddler-speak, lifting her mermaid doll to Collette in offering. Collette's gaze swept past the child as if she weren't there, making Morley's chest tighten with sorrow. It was the one internal battle Collette would never win. Her discomfort around children.

Collette's focus remained fixed on the house as James appeared in the front door.

"Dr. Scott! Perfect timing. Coffee's ready, and I brought a dozen donuts for you and the Mister." James peered around her. "Is he expected soon?"

"Morley's not coming. Family emergency."

"Oh no. That's a shame. It's such a big day for you both," he said, the little girl shyly wrapping her arms around her father's leg. "Oh, as you can see, I've had to bring my little helper along. She's got the sniffles and couldn't go to daycare. Mackenzie, can you say hi?"

Mackenzie slid further behind her dad, her earlier self-confidence gone. Collette didn't notice. Her attention was on something she'd noticed through the living room window. "The river rock on the fireplace looks darker than I remember," she said, starting up the steps. James scooped Mackenzie off the stoop and followed Collette inside.

"Just the morning light," James assured. "Wait until you see what they've done with the kitchen backsplash—"

Their voices faded as the three of them disappeared into

the house, plunging Morley into a restless yearning to be with his wife.

Through the triple-paned windows, he caught glimpses of them meandering from room to room, their lips moving soundlessly behind the thick log walls. But that was a product of his own design. He'd specified every detail of the home's soundproofing—the specialized chinking between the massive logs, the acoustically engineered windows, even the insulated core of each interior door—and today's visit proved the cabin was indeed a fortress against noise.

After what seemed like an eternity, James and Mackenzie emerged from the house and were on their way. Finally Collette was alone.

Finding himself unexpectedly nervous about seeing his wife after four lonely years, Morley crossed the driveway and peered inside the narrow window to the left of the front door. When he couldn't immediately spot her, he tested the door handle, finding it unlocked. As he let himself inside, the smells of rough-hewn timber, fresh paint, and lilies hit him all at once. But it was the aroma of freshly brewed coffee that pulled him toward the kitchen on the lake side of the house, where he hoped to find Collette.

"Hello!" he called as he walked, the dense log walls muffling his voice.

No response.

He stopped at the bottom of the grand curved staircase. "Hi darling, I'm here!"

Silence.

The floor plan they'd chosen for their dream home boasted an open-concept design with as few interior walls as possible. The kitchen and dining room had their own defined space behind a massive wood-burning fireplace in the center of the great room, and when he passed by the cozy fire into the dining area, his heart fluttered. There, out on the deck beyond the tall French doors, was Collette.

"Of course you're outside," he said brightly. The deck was the first place he would have ventured, too. They'd always contended it was the best feature of their lakeside oasis.

He kept his eyes on Collette as he approached the doors. She stood stock still, holding a cup of steaming coffee as she gazed at the placid lake. Morley quietly opened one of the elegant panels and stepped outside, the door whispering shut behind him. In a few seconds, he would be holding his wife in his arms again. If only all grieving people could experience the same joy.

"Hello, darling," he said, moving to a spot a couple of feet behind her and to the right.

She didn't respond. Morley assumed she must've had her earbuds in. He tried again, louder this time. "I thought I might find you here."

Still, she didn't move. It was so odd. Was she that wrapped up in her thoughts?

Rather than tapping her shoulder and making her spill her coffee, he cleared his throat and eased up beside her. He studied her striking profile. Her angular but elegant nose. Her full lips. She tucked a strand of dark, shoulder-length hair behind her ear, revealing the only earrings she ever wore—plain gold hoops. Morley noted the absence of earbuds as he leaned one elbow on the railing in Collette's full view. "Well, now I'm starting to think you're ignoring me." He laughed.

Again, she didn't acknowledge him. She just breathed out a contented sigh, setting her cup on the wide railing, placing both hands on either side.

Something was wrong. Terribly wrong.

Morley reached out and put his hand on Collette's, reeling back in horror when his hand *passed through* hers—as if she didn't exist. As if *he* didn't exist.

He stumbled backward and crashed onto the deck with a thud. Collette merely tilted her head—as if she'd heard a small animal moving in the trees—then drifted back to her thoughts. Morley pressed his fist against his mouth to trap a sob that would fracture the silence. Not that Collette would hear him.

He struggled to his feet on wobbly legs, his hand going to his mouth again, rubbing it, trying to piece together what it all meant.

"You really can't hear me, can you?" he croaked. "Or see me."

Collette lifted her coffee cup and turned, bringing her face inches from his. For a heartbeat, he thought their eyes connected. Then her gaze sliced through him, empty of recognition, devoid of love—just a cold, unseeing stare.

Her eyes lifted to the house and she smiled, beholding the magnificent structure in front of her. She took a sip of coffee and continued toward the house, Morley needlessly dodging out of her way as she passed.

With the deck door closed and Morley left to himself, he descended the stairs and ambled over the newly sodded lawn, across the small beach, and to the end of their private dock. He shook his head in disbelief as he sat down on one of the two Adirondack chairs facing the lake.

"What just happened?" he said, clearly hearing his own voice, wondering why it hadn't been audible to Collette.

He thought back to the little girl, Mackenzie, knowing with certainty that she'd seen him. She'd *waved* to him. She'd shown him her doll.

"Can only children see me on a timeblink?"

As if sent to test the theory, a yellow canoe carrying two passengers drifted into view. Morley didn't recognize the man and a woman as residents of the lake and guessed they were just visiting. The man raised his hand, saying a quick 'hello.'

"Hi!" Morley said, waving back. "Beautiful day for a paddle."

The woman laughed. "Wish I wasn't so useless at it! It's so much harder than I thought it would be."

"Well, from here, it looks like you're doing just fine," Morley said as the canoe shifted, awkwardly presenting their backs to him.

"See what I mean?" she yelled over her shoulder. "Completely useless!"

"You got, this babe. Try to keep the paddle more vertical," the man said.

As they floated away from him, Morley called out, "Enjoy the rest of your paddle. It gets easier, trust me!"

They thanked him and kept going in a zigzag path away from him. He laughed to himself, remembering that exact scenario when he and Collette first got their canoe. It had taken several weeks for them to find their rhythm.

Once the couple was out of sight, Morley relaxed, though still rattled about his encounter with Collette. Or rather, his *non*-encounter with her. Why had he been a ghost to his wife but perfectly visible to everyone else?

Back in his office a few minutes later, Morley was exhausted from the rush of emotions he'd experienced the last hour. He should've been happy that he'd navigated another successful timeblink. He should've been celebrating the proof that the talisman's power was real and that he had full control of it. Instead, he was miserable and unsettled, and the more he racked his brain to figure out why he'd been invisible to his wife, the more miserable and unsettled he became.

There was another troubling detail playing on his mind— the significance of the dates he'd been able to travel to…and the ones he had not.

He would have to flesh out this nagging thought after a good night's sleep. Right now, he felt nauseous, and it occurred to him that his last "meal" had been at noon: a raspberry-filled donut and a black coffee. The combination of sugar and caffeine had given him an instant energy boost, but after a few hours, he'd suffered a spectacular mid-afternoon crash and had to force himself to power through his rounds at the end of the day. He would need to pick something up on the way home.

Locking his office door a few moments later, his mind went back to the dates. "Aha," he said, dropping his keys into his jacket pocket. It was then he knew his next timeblink would be to February 12, 1969—a year before his birth. If he failed that attempt, he could deduce with near certainty that it was impossible to timeblink to a date preceding one's own existence.

Chapter Eight

After an uneventful drive home in light traffic—even his annoying stalker was absent tonight—the hallway outside Morley's penthouse greeted him with an unexpected smell...a delightfully rich and savory aroma that made his mouth water. Was that stew? Chicken pot pie? He pictured Mrs. Bennett next door, who hadn't cooked a meal since her husband died six months ago. "Well, good for her. She's finally dusted off her cookbook."

Inside his apartment, the smell of food was oddly more intense, but he dismissed it as one of the mild drawbacks of condo living. Smelling other people's culinary efforts. Thinking nothing more of it, he dropped his keys into the bowl by the door and kicked off his shoes, still in quiet heartache about his encounter with Collette.

"Get it together, man. Without the talisman, you wouldn't have seen her at all," he said to the empty room, carrying a paper bag of takeout food to the kitchen. It felt like a guilty secret in his hand. When was the last time he'd eaten a nutritious meal? Or visited the gym downstairs? Between time-blinking and the unnerving stalker situation, his carefully cultivated health routine had gone completely sideways.

When he entered the kitchen a moment later, he stopped dead in his tracks, the bag slipping from his hands and landing on the floor with a soft plunk.

Standing at the island in the middle of the room was Syd —the bartender from The Merryport—looking for all the world like she belonged there. In her hand, she held what looked like one of her classic martinis, garnished with two olives on a bamboo stick. Her expression was calm, almost expectant, as if Morley's arrival had been right on schedule.

He opened his mouth to speak, but the words froze on his tongue.

Syd stepped forward, pressing the chilled cocktail into his hand. "Drink first, questions later," she said with a wink. She bent down and collected the bag of food from the floor. Her nose wrinkled as she peeked inside. "Really? A meatball sub?"

Morley remained still, holding his delicate cocktail, trying to process why his neighborhood bartender had broken into his apartment and commandeered his kitchen to cook a meal. While pots bubbled away on the stove behind Syd, Morley hoped he wasn't losing his mind. Had he invited her over and forgotten? He shuddered. The idea of Syd entering his apartment without his permission was one thing. The prospect of memory loss was quite another. While nothing about it made sense, if he was being honest, he found her strange presence mildly comforting, given what he'd just been through with Collette.

"You're probably wondering why I'm here, preparing your favorite dinner."

"The thought had crossed my mind." He nodded to the oven. "Braised short ribs?"

"Of course."

Morley couldn't recall ever mentioning his favorite entrée to Syd, but he supposed he had at some point in the last four years of their acquaintance.

"I'll tell you all about it in a few minutes. Just let me finish things up, and we'll chat over dinner. You'll thank me later for sparing you from that disgusting sub. God, Morley, you really must be in a state."

Her casual demeanor ruffled him a little, as did the subtle variances in her appearance and character. She seemed less guarded somehow. More refined. He observed fine laugh lines around her eyes and mouth that he'd never noticed. Had they always been there, masked by the muted lighting at The Merryport? Or was it just that he'd never looked closely enough? Perhaps it was because her face was devoid of her usual heavier eye shadow and pink lipstick. Maybe she only wore makeup at work.

Nearly forgetting he was holding a martini, Morley finally took a sip. It was perfect, exactly the way Syd prepared them at The Merryport. He set it on the polished quartz countertop and cleared his throat. "Don't you work tonight?"

"Nope."

"I almost didn't recognize you out of your work clothes."

Syd glanced down at her outfit, a pair of faded jeans and a magenta cashmere turtleneck sweater cinched at the waist with a belt—a departure from her black Merryport tee and leggings.

"You look nice," Morley added, thinking what an understatement that was. She was stunning. Not too slim, curves in all the right places, intense blue eyes that could melt an iceberg. A thought danced across his mind that if she wasn't already hitched to an attractive firefighter…

Stop it! his conscience snapped. *You've just been with your wife.*

Syd pulled a black scrunchie from her long blonde hair and slipped it over her wrist. "Thanks. Wish I could say the same about you. For shit's sake, Morley, when was the last time you slept? Or shaved?"

His hand flew up to his chin, discovering a couple of days' worth of growth. He was shocked by his oversight, though it explained why his assistant gave him a second look when he'd arrived at the office this morning. Still. Who was Syd to break into his apartment and start slinging insults at him?

"I'm sorry," she added. "This is probably super weird for you. I need to remind myself this is our first meeting."

"First meeting?"

"Look, why don't you go take a shower and freshen up? I should have dinner on the table by the time you're finished, and I'll explain everything the best I can."

The thought of washing the day off appealed to Morley. Maybe when he came back, he would discover it had all been a dream, and Syd would be gone. Yet, on some level, he knew that wouldn't be the case, given the string of peculiar events that had been occurring lately. *Oh god.* Did timeblinking have anything to do with this?

He caught Syd's eye, and a glimmer of understanding passed between them. "Go on," she said. "I haven't got all night."

Chapter Nine

The bedroom mirror reflected a transformed man.

With a quiet sense of curiosity rippling beneath his skin, Morley admired his carefully chosen dark jeans and burgundy button-down shirt left open at the neck. He slid his thin leather gloves over his hands, his mind still reeling from the surreal events of the past few hours: His timeblink to Jackson Beach. His invisibility to Collette. The unexpected woman in his kitchen.

As he padded down the hall, the smell of simmering meat and vegetables reminded him of Sunday roasts with Collette, and he couldn't shake the feeling that he was somehow betraying her—even if he hadn't invited Syd into his home.

He entered the dining area, now ravenous, noticing that Syd had been busy in his absence. A soft contemporary melody drifted through the room, setting a slightly contemplative mood. The table was a picture of elegance—his finest dinnerware laid out with precision, a glass of red wine at one setting, a bottle of sparkling water at the other. His eyes went to the credenza, where his photo albums and loose pictures sat in neat piles. He caught Syd's gaze, noticing a flicker of guilt.

"I hope you don't mind," she said, gesturing to the photos. "I was just tidying up a bit."

Morley nodded, unsure how to respond. The casual way she moved about his apartment, the ease with which she'd accessed his personal belongings—it all felt oddly familiar, yet also completely foreign. This wasn't the same Syd he knew from The Merryport, always maintaining a friendly but professional distance. This Syd exuded an air of intimacy that both intrigued and unnerved him.

He waited until Syd sat down at the dining table before taking a seat across from her, the silence between them swirling with unspoken questions. Morley raised his glass of wine. "To the chef. This looks amazing."

Syd picked up her glass and tapped Morley's. "Thank you. I hope it tastes as good."

Without a further word, they both dug into their meal. Morley couldn't help but be distracted by his companion, stealing glances at her as they ate and admiring the way the soft lighting accentuated her golden highlights and elegant cheekbones. Again, he noticed the faint lines around her eyes and mouth. He found these subtle markers of time alluring, adding a depth to her beauty that he hadn't appreciated before.

Amidst the gentle clatter of cutlery and the lilting music, Morley realized he'd all but forgotten about his disturbing encounter with Collette. And he couldn't deny a sense of contentment in Syd's company.

As he savored some of the most delicious short ribs he'd ever eaten, he pondered the events of the past few days. It was obvious that the talisman, the timeblinking, and now Syd's unexpected visit were all connected. But how?

With the edge taken off of his appetite and his curiosity piqued, he set his utensils down to speak, but Syd beat him to it.

"You have no clue what's going on, do you?" she asked, her voice calm yet laced with excitement.

Morley leaned back in his chair and folded his arms. "Pretty sure I understand the situation perfectly."

Syd reached into her mock turtleneck and drew out an item that made Morley's breath hitch. A dragonfly talisman. *His* dragonfly talisman. His hand shot up to his chest, where he could feel his own pendant hanging in its rightful place. Relief coursed through his body, but he was nonetheless astonished by the duplicate piece.

"I presume our talismans are one and the same," he said.

"They are."

"How did you get it?"

"You might not believe me."

"I'm all ears."

Syd licked her lips and looked down at her half-eaten plate of food. "From you," she said, lifting her gaze to meet his eyes. "I got it from you."

Morley could only stare blankly at his visitor.

Over a song about someone being in love on a Friday, Syd said, "I can't tell you the circumstances, but just know that in September of this year, you will give me the talisman as a gift."

Skepticism painted Morley's face. "It belonged to my wife and had been in her family for years. I can't see myself just giving it away."

"You can, and you will."

"Why?"

"Because you've entrusted me with the power for a reason."

"I barely know you."

"That's true. You don't know me very well *now*."

Morley pressed his lips together, waiting for Syd to go on.

"Look, all I can say is that in the coming days, you'll begin to understand, as I do, the dangers of letting this power fall into the wrong hands."

"What's that supposed to mean?"

"I can't tell you. Not now."

"Why?"

"Because we have a history, and I don't want to fuck it up."

"History? The only history we have is my monthly visits to your pub."

"Do you really believe that?"

"I don't know what to believe."

"Try this. You *will* give me the talisman, and do you know why I'm so certain of it?"

Morley shrugged as if to say *You're going to tell me anyway.*

Syd picked up her fork and stabbed a roasted carrot. "Because I've been timeblinking with it for four years."

After they'd finished their meal and carried the dishes to the kitchen, Morley poured himself another glass of wine and offered Syd a coffee. She declined, helping herself to another bottle of sparkling water from the fridge. They headed into the living room where Syd took a seat on the couch. As Morley sank into his favorite armchair, Syd pointed to his gloves. "Those aren't necessary. I won't turn to stone or die if you touch me."

It shocked Morley that—besides knowing the term 'time-blinking'—Syd was also privy to this extremely private fact about him. The fact that he'd been wearing gloves in public ever since Collette died *not* because he was afraid of germs but because he'd developed an unshakable belief that anyone he touched—particularly those he cared about— would meet an untimely demise. He'd never told another soul about it.

"Besides," Syd went on, "we never made skin-to-skin

contact with each other in our natural timeline. That's why you can see me right now. I'd be invisible to you otherwise."

"Invisible?" Morley said, his eyes going wide. "Is…is that why Collette couldn't see or hear me when I visited her today?" he sputtered.

Syd nodded solemnly. "In fact, not only are you a ghost to anyone you've ever physically touched, the same applies to yourself." She grinned. "It's a total trip being able to spy on yourself, unseen."

Morley stared at her for a couple of beats.

"How do you know all this?"

"You gave me—or rather *will* give the 2019 version of me —a crash course on April twentieth, the date of my first timeblink."

"I don't understand how you got involved in this," Morley said, nursing his wine. "Do you have anything to do with the man following me?"

"What man?"

Morley's brows raised briefly. "Obviously not."

"Who's following you?"

"It doesn't matter. Probably my imagination."

"Come on, spit it out. What's going on?"

"Honestly? I don't know. This shadow appeared the day after my first timeblink. He hasn't threatened me or tried to make contact otherwise. He's just been…watching me. It's disturbing."

"No shit," Syd replied. "Fortunately, you don't have to worry about him."

"I beg your pardon?"

"Ignore him."

"Easy for you to say."

"Remember, I'm here from 2023. I'd be willing to stake my life on the fact that he won't be a problem for you."

"Well, that's a relief."

Syd looked at him sideways. "Was that sarcasm?"

"Why are you here, Syd?"

"Everything will make sense soon. Trust me. In the meantime, what exactly have you learned about timeblinking?"

"If you're from 2023, shouldn't you already know all that?"

"By the time I meet up with you on my first timeblink in April, you're basically a pro. Right now, you're just figuring it out. If you tell me what you've learned, I might be able to give you some tips to navigate the whole thing a little more efficiently."

Unable to argue with that logic, Morley gave her the rundown of his timeblinking efforts over the last five days.

"Impressive," Syd said. "You have a good grasp of the basics and have already figured out the time specificity hack."

"The what?"

"If you don't want to end up at your desired location at midnight, you have to specify a time of day. Do you also know that the details you recite must follow a certain order?"

"If by that you mean destination, time, and date, then yes. It took some trial and error. Like the revelation that you need to say it all twice."

Syd shook her head. "Not true. You only need to say it once."

"Then what happened on my first attempt to Jackson Beach? I had to say it twice."

"Could've been anything. Maybe your fingers weren't positioned properly the first time. Or you got the order wrong. Or your eyes were closed."

"Your eyes have to be open?"

"Indeed, they do. Yet another bizarre rule of this phenomenon."

"Do I have to be holding my mouth just right, too?"

"Ha, maybe," Syd said. "Listen, I should get going soon."

Not ready for her to leave, Morley thought of another question. "Why must the talisman be held between the fingers for a successful trip? I mean, it's already touching your skin, right?"

"That's one of the things you and I haven't nailed yet. Our best guess is that it creates an energy between the thumb and finger that's necessary for a timeblink."

"Not a bad theory."

"Anything else?"

"As a matter of fact, yes. Have you been able to travel back to a time before you were born?"

"Nope. That's one of the limitations."

"Are there others?"

"I really should go. I'm tired."

The change in subject didn't go unnoticed. "What are the other limitations?" Morley asked again.

"That's it for tonight. In your famous words, 'We should let this play out naturally.'"

"I never said that."

She winked. "You will. Just know that we agreed my first visit would be today and that I shouldn't give you any more details about our 'future history' or about…our friendship."

Not sure how to interpret that, Morley leaned forward and set his glass on the coffee table, a huge white marble slab that Collette had picked out in the late nineties. He clasped his hands between his knees. "So, you've come here from 2023," he said, snickering at the absurdity of the statement, "to treat me to a fantastic dinner and then leave me hanging about our 'future history' that I know nothing about?"

"Sorry, but yes. This is just an introductory timeblink. I'll be back in a few days when you've learned more. In the meantime, don't be tempted to come and see me at The Merryport until your usual second-Friday visit."

"That's three weeks away. You expect me to wait that long?"

"What would you say to me, anyway? That version of Syd has no idea about any of this."

Morley leaned back and scratched his smooth chin. "This is so odd."

"Just carry on doing what you're doing, like nothing out of the ordinary is going on, and we'll talk more next time."

"If by carrying on as usual you mean continue my experimentation with timeblinking, I was going to do that anyway."

"And so you should. The more you know by the next time I come, the better. Have you figured out the skin-contact thing yet?"

"You already told me. No one I've ever touched can see me during a timeblink."

"There's more to it." Syd bit her bottom lip. "I suppose it can't hurt to tell you one more thing. It could save you a lot of trouble."

"Do tell."

"Anything you want to take with you on a timeblink has to be touching your skin. For instance, if you have keys in your pocket, they won't go with you since they're not in direct contact with your skin."

A light went on behind Morley's eyes. "That's why my shoes were missing. Because I was wearing socks."

"Exactly. So, hot tip: don't wear socks when you timeblink. Problem solved."

"Duly noted."

Syd pushed herself up off the couch. "Anyway, I'll finish cleaning the kitchen and get going."

"That's not necessary," Morley said, standing to join her.

"What's not necessary? Cleaning the kitchen?" Syd asked, flashing him a smile. "Or leaving?"

Morley liked this version of Syd. She was feistier. More assertive with him than the Syd at the pub. More familiar. He supposed in another timeline, she *was*.

"As much as I'd like you to stay, you don't need to worry about the mess in the kitchen. You cooked me a five-star meal. The least I can do is clean up."

"I won't argue with that." Syd took hold of the talisman between her forefinger and thumb. "Are you ready for a mindfuck?"

He winced at her word choice.

"Oh, Morley. You're adorable. Are you ready to watch me disappear?"

He nodded, though he'd rather she didn't go.

"Alright. See you in a few days." Syd gave him a cheeky wink. "Return!"

And like that, she vanished.

Morley dropped into his chair. "Mindfuck indeed," he said, his language surprising him. It seemed his time-traveling friend was having an influence on him.

He grabbed his glass and knocked back the last third of his wine, mildly concerned about his new propensity to reach for alcohol to settle his nerves. But what he'd been through would've shaken even the most unflappable person. It was justified.

His thoughts drifted back to Syd. He'd always had a fondness for her, perhaps a little more than he would like to admit, given her longstanding relationship with her handsome firefighter, Cooper. Morley would never step on another man's toes. Still, this encounter gave him pause. Had Syd been flirting with him?

"No way." He shook his head, remembering the calendar behind Syd's bar, the one perpetually open to May 2008. It featured Cooper in all his firefighter glory—tanned and shirtless, axe in hand, flames licking at his glistening torso. "I'm reading way too much into it."

Twenty minutes later, still breathless from the whirlwind that was Syd, Morley tossed and turned in bed, his groin betraying every fiber of his good senses. Senses that told him Syd had simply been in a playful mood, perhaps even enjoying Morley's fumbling confusion as he pieced everything together.

Syd Brixton.

The attractive cocktail artist at his favorite pub. The pub he and Collette used to visit…

He groaned and sat bolt upright in bed, guilt pushing down on his heart like a brick. He'd seen his wife today. Close enough to touch, yet impossibly out of reach.

"You're allowed to think about someone else," he reminded himself in the stillness. "Collette's gone. And you can't do a darned thing about it."

He flopped onto his back and stared at a strip of moonlight on his ceiling, his mind wandering back to Syd.

She'd called him *adorable*.

"I mean, she's not wrong," he joked. "She may have a buff firefighter at home, but I'm not exactly an ogre."

No, he thought. Not an ogre at all. Women—and even some men—were constantly vying for his affections. He'd been on several dates since Collette's death, but nothing ever stuck, as much as his companions had wanted to continue seeing him. Morley would invariably let them down gently, stating he wasn't ready, assuring them it was *him*, not them. Which was true. He'd begun to wonder if he would *ever* be ready. That was, until Syd had descended on his apartment, swept him away with a gourmet meal, and twirled out of there in the blink of an eye.

Even if he couldn't have Syd, her presence had stirred something deep within him. The desire for connection. A sudden, burning *need* for connection.

But there it was—that old, sabotaging thought again. The one that reminded him he was cursed. That anyone he loved would turn to stone under his touch.

No. He could not, *would not* get close to Syd, or anyone else for that matter. It was his last thought before sleep pulled him under.

Chapter Ten

An unexpected lightness filled Morley's heart when he woke before sunrise the next day. As he poured a cup of coffee, he let out a contented sigh, knowing he had the whole weekend to continue his timeblinking trials. Despite the invisibility issue weighing on his mind, he was eager to unravel every nuance of this extraordinary power. Maybe then he could figure out a way to save Collette's life.

He carried his coffee into the living room and took a seat on the couch where Syd had sat the night before. He clicked his dictation app open. "January 19, 2019, 6:53 a.m. Thanks to a friend visiting me from 2023," he said, the words beginning to sound normal to him, "I have some new insight into the timeblinking phenomenon." He paused to slurp his coffee.

"Not only did Syd tell me that skin contact plays a critical role, but she also confirmed my nagging suspicion that a person can't travel back to a time before their birth. But what about the future? Does this same limitation apply? Does it mean that one cannot timeblink beyond their death?"

Though unsettled by the implication, his need to prove or disprove the theory drove him forward. He would start with something manageable—a week into the future. He would go to his cabin at Sandalwood Lake, where he could enjoy privacy and the luxury of his computer to confirm the date and time.

"Or…" he said, picking up his cell phone, "I could just bring this along."

With the talisman in one hand and his phone in the other, he recited his destination, this time aiming to arrive in the evening.

"819 Chapman Road, nine o'clock, January 26, 2019."

At once, he was standing in front of his cabin, his warm breath forming billowy white clouds in the chilled air. Something wasn't right, though. Not only was there smoke puffing out of his chimney, but the sky—though overcast—was far too light for a Pacific Northwest evening in mid-January. It felt more like morning.

He hurriedly raised his phone to check the time and date, but instead of seeing his usual home screen, a garbled jumble of glitchy lines, colors, and pixels had taken over his display. The device vibrated erratically in his hand as if struggling to maintain its digital composure, while a medley of distorted electronic chirps and beeps screeched from the speaker.

As he fumbled to shut it down, the screen went black on its own. He groaned. However, a fried phone wasn't his biggest problem. Who was inside his house keeping the fire stoked? His heart leapt. Had Syd broken in again?

Ready for a confrontation, he climbed the steps to his door but stopped short of punching in his code. A smile washed over his face with the realization that his intruder probably wasn't Syd at all, but Morley himself, a week in his future.

He hadn't anticipated this potential hiccup of him already being here, though he really should've prepared for it. He enjoyed spending weekends at the lake in the dead of winter when the seasonal residents tended to stay away. He smiled to himself again. It didn't matter that his future self was here. According to Syd, he would be invisible to him anyway.

Emboldened by the revelation, he keyed in his door code and quietly let himself inside. As he made his way through the foyer toward the living room, he indeed heard his own voice, muffled, as if in a closed room. Or outside, perhaps, on the deck.

Morley crept around the corner and was halfway across the living room when he abruptly stopped. Through the French doors leading to the deck, he glimpsed not one but two people occupying his matching Adirondack chairs. They wore knit caps, sweaters, and puffy vests, and were warming their hands over the gas fire table, looking the epitome of the West Coast lifestyle. Steam escaped from two insulated coffee mugs that sat invitingly on a small table between them.

As he tried to make out his visitor's identity, he heard a muted laugh.

A woman's laugh.

Morley ducked behind the tall steampunk bookcase he'd splurged on last year and peered around it. "What on Earth?" he murmured, though not surprised at all to discover that it was his friendly neighborhood bartender, Syd, enjoying his future self's company. She laughed again as future Morley stood up, collected the mugs, and turned to the patio doors.

Morley dropped back behind the bookcase as his slightly older self entered the house.

"I'll be right back," he clearly heard himself say.

Once the door was closed and his doppelganger busied himself refilling the mugs, Morley stepped out from his cover, feeling like he had nothing to lose. "Good to see you enjoying yourself," he said as his twin poured the contents of a teapot into Syd's mug.

Future Morley paused in mid-pour as though he'd heard a noise.

Uh oh.

But then he shook his head, apparently satisfied that he'd

heard nothing. He finished pouring Syd's tea and then filled his own mug with coffee.

Moving closer to his oblivious twin, Morley pondered whether he would be invisible to Syd, too. And on the heels of that thought, he wondered which version of Syd was sitting on his deck right now: present-day Syd or Syd from the future?

As his handsome twin stepped back onto the deck in the cool January morning, Morley had all but convinced himself that the woman sitting out there was the time-traveling Syd. There was no way her present self would look that comfortable in Morley's company a week in the future. They just weren't that friendly with each other.

Yet.

With nothing left to do but confirm the date on his computer, he recalled, alarmingly, that he hadn't seen a strange car out front when he'd arrived.

His skin prickled.

Had Syd stayed overnight?

No. It had to mean that she'd taken a taxi here. Or that future Morley had picked her up.

But then a new revelation surfaced that made him laugh. "Of course there's no car. She timeblinked here."

Feeling relieved but also a little disappointed, he dashed over to his computer and logged in. Sure enough, the date read January 26, 2019, 9:06 a.m. So, there it was: proof he could timeblink to the future and furthermore that he would need to specify a.m. or p.m. when stating the time.

As he looked over his shoulder at the pair on the deck, he wondered: What was Syd doing at his lakeside sanctuary? A sanctuary that, until today, he'd only ever shared with Collette.

Chapter Eleven

It turned out the allure of revisiting the future was too strong for Morley to resist.

In the hours following his timeblink to Sandalwood Lake, he uncharacteristically skipped his normal Saturday morning walk to The Bold & Bean, didn't eat breakfast or lunch, and cancelled a much-anticipated dinner date with an old acquaintance from med school.

Instead, he'd fired up his phone and spent the first half of the day documenting increasingly desperate attempts to reach the future. Starting ambitiously with his ninety-ninth year—hoping to discover a world of extraordinary medical advances and harmony among his fellow humans—he found himself unable to timeblink to 2069. Working backward through the decades proved equally futile. Each failed attempt to reach 2059, 2049, and even 2039 left him shaken and exhausted, and at noon, he curled up on the couch and fell into a fitful slumber.

At 2:15, Morley awoke foggy-headed but eager to continue his experiments. After freshening up, he returned to his living room and signed into VoxLog.

"If it's true that one cannot timeblink beyond their own lifespan," he said, "then today's developments would suggest that I don't even make it to seventy years of age."

He knew he should stop now. What good could possibly come from discovering one's own death date? Yet he couldn't resist further testing.

When he couldn't timeblink beyond October 2019, his gut twisted with dread.

He peered out at the darkened January sky, where ashen clouds drifted past a glowing crescent moon. He picked up his phone and recorded a worrying thought. "Does this mean I'll die in September, eight months from now?"

He paused the recording and leaned back in his chair, staring at the coffered ceiling overhead. Collette had disliked the formal design of that ceiling in their ultra-modern apartment. Morley, on the other hand, had always loved the splash of old-world charm to offset all the polished chrome and gleaming white surfaces throughout.

"What would you have done in this situation, my dear?" he asked the empty room. "I know what you *wouldn't* have done. You wouldn't have accepted this morbid conclusion. You would've kept testing until you had proof."

With that thought, he sat up and began working methodically backward through September, hope soaring when he successfully timeblinked to September twelfth.

He stood outside his cabin at 10:30 in the evening, where warm lighting glowed cozily inside. He didn't bother going in. Instead, he peered in a window, spotting himself engaged in conversation with Syd in the living room, Syd seated on the couch facing the hearth while future Morley paced the floor, half a glass of red wine in his hand. They didn't appear as cheerful as the last time he'd seen them together. They seemed tense. A disagreement, perhaps?

A pang of curiosity about Syd's constant presence pulled at his thoughts, but not enough to outweigh his desperate need to pinpoint the limitations of future travel. He returned to his present after the requisite four minutes and forty-four seconds.

So that was it, then. September twelfth was the final day he was able to timeblink to the future. Was it also his last day of life?

With the truth within his grasp, he gathered his courage and resumed his testing.

Starting at 11:59 p.m. on September thirteenth, he worked his way backward in one-hour increments until his attempt to eight o'clock left him standing outside his cabin amidst a tempestuous coastal rainstorm.

This time, the house looked dark and empty with no sign of either of his vehicles parked outside. "He must be in the city." As soon as the words left his lips, a realization came to him: of course he was in the city. It was the second Friday of the month—his usual visit to The Merryport.

"I suppose if a person is going to meet his maker, it might as well be at his favorite pub."

Now he knew where he would be and at what time it would happen: sometime between eight and nine p.m.. Now, all he had to do was go there.

Chapter Twelve

Dressed in a long, gray raincoat and wool scarf, Morley waited under an umbrella a short distance away from The Merryport's entrance. He doubted his future self would even visit the pub in this weather with rain pulsing sideways and wind stripping the trees of their final leaves. Thus, he was surprised when the future version of himself pulled into the parking lot at 7:28 and dashed into the pub.

He was tempted to follow his doomed self inside where it was warm and dry, but he didn't want people to recognize him and become alarmed when they saw two versions of him. No, it would be best to wait outside, and if his future self didn't emerge by nine o'clock, he would know he'd died inside. And for proof, he could simply wait for an ambulance—or the coroner—to arrive.

Thirty-five minutes later, with his shoes and lower half of his pants soaked through, Morley straightened when he heard the roar of an engine. He watched with interest as a black late-model pickup truck slid to a stop in a loading zone across the street from the pub, its throaty engine revving obnoxiously. Probably someone's ride home.

A few more minutes passed.

He didn't think it possible, but the rain intensified, pelting his umbrella and running off of it in a torrent.

Through the deluge, he watched a couple, barely in their twenties, emerge from the pub. The young man opened a large black umbrella and centered it over the girl's head. They stopped to lock lips for an unnatural amount of time, their heads moving passionately in the downpour. Despite himself, Morley smiled.

Just then, another person emerged from the pub, but Morley was too fascinated by the young couple, wondering when they would come up for air, to take much notice. When they finally parted a minute later and zigzagged around puddles to a nearby crosswalk, Morley recalled with fondness all those years ago when he and Collette would—

Suddenly he saw—and heard—the waiting truck peel away from the curb, its tires spinning on the wet pavement, the engine roaring even louder. The tires found their traction and the truck lurched forward, the driver not even attempting to stop before crashing into the couple in the crosswalk, sending them flying. Morley gasped as the truck continued toward The Merryport's entrance at full speed.

With his doctor's instinct kicking in, Morley rushed toward the young couple as the truck hit the pub's brick wall with enough force to shake the ground.

Before Morley could reach the couple, three more people appeared out of the blue, one of them shouting that she was an ER doctor and instructing bystanders to direct traffic around them. While the doctor focused on the victims, Morley's gaze went to a woman standing next to the truck, screaming hysterically. As he got closer, he witnessed a sight so horrific it made his knees buckle: pinned between the truck's grille and the wall of The Merryport Pub was Morley *himself*, his eyes rolling back in his head while streams of blood gushed from his mouth and nose.

Morley stumbled back and fell in a puddle. He barely

registered a young woman helping him up a few moments later, nor that the woman had handed him his umbrella. Without a word, he shuffled away from the scene, finding a spot between two cars in the parking lot. He slithered down, out of sight, shivering and soaked to the bone. He honestly didn't care. The image of his own broken body would haunt him forever...however brief forever might be.

Sitting in the relentless icy rain, he began to cry. Two, three, maybe even ten minutes passed. He didn't know.

With his guttural sobs turning into retching, he dragged himself to his hands and knees and vomited. No one came to console him. No one could hear him over the din of the storm, the frantic people, and the wail of approaching sirens.

Peering out from behind the car, he watched the truck back away as his twin collapsed into the arms of bystanders. Among them were Tad from The Merryport and one of the bank tellers who frequented the pub on Fridays with her coworkers. They laid his body down gingerly on the wet ground as another woman stepped up and held a happy-face umbrella over his blood-streaked face.

Blinking back hot tears, Morley watched Syd emerge from the crowd and dash over to his broken form. She knelt and leaned her ear next to his mouth as if to listen to what Morley was trying to say, and a moment later—

Morley landed in his living room on hands and knees, his wet clothes clinging to his body as he gasped for air. He let out a guttural sob and rolled onto his back. He didn't know how he'd gotten there. He hadn't even touched the talisman.

He lay there for ten minutes, trembling and whimpering until his discomfort compelled him to get up. On shaky legs, he stumbled to the bathroom and cranked on the shower as hot as it would go, stripping off his wet clothes. He bawled under the hot stream for five minutes. Then bent over and threw up again.

Once he was sure he wasn't going to vomit anymore, he turned off the shower, toweled off, and wrapped himself in his fluffy white robe, which had been warming on the towel heater. It did little to comfort him as the image of his crushed body tortured his thoughts.

Morley stalked listlessly into the living room and went straight to his liquor cabinet. There, he drew out a bottle of fine Irish Whisky and filled a crystal tumbler three-quarters full, knocking it back in one gulp without even sitting down. He filled it again and walked over to his floor-to-ceiling window overlooking the harbor.

None of this mattered anymore. The executive eighteenth-floor penthouse. The luxury cars. The cabin at the lake. They were meaningless. He was going to die in eight months, alone but for a few kindhearted strangers.

And Syd. Always Syd.

After his second glass of whisky, numbness began to creep in. Numbness of hands, of face, of mind. He guzzled the rest of the liquor straight from the bottle and then shuffled down the hallway to his bedroom, where he shed his robe and crawled between his crisp white sheets. His smart lights dimmed in stages, sensing his presence in bed.

Before he knew it, he'd drifted off.

Chapter Thirteen

It was two in the morning when she arrived—at least that's what the blurred numbers on Morley's clock suggested, though he couldn't be certain.

In his groggy, booze-induced stupor, Morley saw her silhouette against the backdrop of the city lights, moving about his bedroom, almost floating as she placed a glass on his night table. Water? Whisky? Poison? He didn't care. It didn't matter. His grisly death permeated his every thought.

"Collette?" he mumbled as every synapse in his brain protested. This was not his wife.

He struggled to focus on the form darting around his room like a pixie. Was she real? A dream? Sleep claimed him once again.

He awoke, perhaps a few minutes later, perhaps hours, to a warm body molded perfectly to his own. He flopped an arm over her waist out of habit. *Collette*. God, how he'd missed her.

She removed his arm and flipped over, taking his hands into hers. "You poor thing. I'm here now."

Her voice was soothing. Familiar. But it did not belong to his wife.

He blinked twice. "Syd?"

"Yes."

"What are you doing here?"

At once, Syd was upright, pulling off her t-shirt and throwing it aside. In the glow of the moonlight, Morley drank in the beauty of her. The soft curve of her hips; her pert, ample breasts; her bouncy golden curls cascading over lean shoulders.

She reached down, her touch making him hard. Even Morley was surprised. He'd had a lot to drink. But it had been such a long time since he'd been intimate with anyone, and the physiological hurdle was no match for his primal desire. He *needed* this.

Syd's touch ignited sensations Morley hadn't experienced in years. In his haze of grief and whiskey, her presence felt like a lifeline, tethering him to the present.

"Shh," she whispered. "I know what you found out. But right now, you're very much alive. Let me remind you what that feels like."

Her words sent a shiver through him as his hands explored her feminine curves. He marveled at the miracle of human touch, of the pure eroticism of skin on skin. In the dim light, Syd's eyes smoldered with passion, certainly, but beneath her gaze lay something more profound. Understanding. Connection. And even deeper still, a possibility that both thrilled and terrified Morley—the possibility of love.

Syd straddled him, her honey-blonde locks framing her face like a halo. She guided him inside her. As she sank down, enclosing him in her warmth, Morley let out a moan. It had been so long since he'd been able to enjoy such raw passion.

Their bodies undulated in perfect rhythm, each thrust taking Morley further away from his troubles. His hands roamed over Syd's breasts and hips and traced the curve of her spine as she arched under his touch.

"You're not alone," she whispered.

At those words, Morley felt a dam break within him. Tears

streamed off his face and onto the pillow, a release of pent-up emotion he hadn't allowed himself to feel in years.

Despite Morley's sudden flash of despair, their rhythm intensified, Syd's breath now coming in urgent gasps. Morley felt the familiar tightening in his groin, the edge of bliss approaching.

"I'm going to come," he murmured.

Before Syd could respond, Morley exploded in a burst of ecstasy.

As their profound pleasure gave way to a gentle, pulsing afterglow, Morley clung to Syd like a drowning man to a life raft. To him, their culmination had been less a moment of passion and more a catharsis, a purging of fear and loneliness. Peace settled over him like a warm hug.

With Syd's head tucked under his chin, his thoughts bounced between gratitude that this woman had shown up when she did and self-loathing for having become the very thing he despised—a man who'd betrayed another man's relationship. Worse still, in the thrill of the moment, he hadn't thought to use a condom. Hadn't even asked Syd if she was protected.

His final waking thought was a promise to himself: No matter how many days he had left on this Earth, he would not spend them so irresponsibly.

Chapter Fourteen

orley's eyes fluttered open to daylight, his head pounding with the remnants of the previous night's whiskey binge. He reached out, expecting to feel Syd's warm body beside him, but his hand met only cool, rumpled sheets.

"Syd?"

Silence answered him.

As the fog of sleep lifted, snippets of the previous night teased the edges of his mind. Syd's silhouette in the moonlight. Her dewy skin. The way she'd moved as one with him. And the hazy details he *could* remember stirred something within his depths, a longing he thought he'd abandoned years ago.

He sat up, wincing at the throb behind his forehead, cursing the dryness of his mouth. His hand went for the glass of water on his nightstand, pausing in mid-reach. He hadn't remembered putting it there. But then again, he didn't remember much.

He gulped the water down, all the while scanning the room for evidence that Syd had been there. No discarded clothing on the floor. No purse. No shoes. He picked up the pillow next to his, finding not a single blonde hair. Even the subtle floral scent of her perfume had vanished from the room.

Grunting, he swung his legs over the side of the bed and stood, stretching his aching muscles. He meandered through the condo, knowing it would be futile, but nonetheless checking every room for signs that Syd had been there. The bathroom was as he'd left it, holding no damp towels or stray blonde hair anywhere. The spare bedrooms, den, office, and living room were equally empty, and nothing had been disturbed in the kitchen.

After completing his search, he was more than convinced that the night's events had been nothing more than a drunken reverie—a fantasy his mind had concocted to cope with his looming inescapable destiny. Knowing it had only been a dream left him with a conflicting sense of relief and disappointment.

He flopped onto the couch. Indeed, if none of it had been real, then he hadn't betrayed the sanctity of Syd and Cooper's relationship. Furthermore, he could take solace in the fact that he wasn't the reckless asshole who'd thrown caution to the wind, potentially risking an unplanned pregnancy or compromising Syd's health. Or his.

Did his own health even matter anymore?

With Herculean effort, Morley dragged himself to the shower. As the hot water flowed over him, he reveled in the memory his encounter with Syd, even if it was a dream. A pang of regret hit him as he realized how little time he had left to truly know her in real life, to explore the connection that Syd herself had sparked between them.

With the steam swirling hypnotically around him, his thoughts wandered to the dinner Syd had prepared two nights ago and her insistence that Morley would give her the talisman in the future. The idea didn't seem so far-fetched anymore. Perhaps she was meant to help him, to use the power of timeblinking to save his life.

As the water hammered at his back, a new thought emerged. Why wait for Syd? He had the power *now*. He could go to The Merryport on that fateful day and find a way to warn himself to leave early. He switched off the water and hopped out of the shower with new optimism. He had the means to change his fate, and maybe even Collette's, too. And he wouldn't wait another moment to launch his assault on destiny.

Morley pulled on a pair of jeans, a gray Merino wool sweater, and a black leather jacket as he dictated his intentions into his audio journal. Exactly how he was going to head off his death wasn't yet clear, but he was certain the universe had granted him this power for a reason.

He clutched the talisman and timeblinked to The Merryport twenty minutes before his gruesome accident.

Disguised in a ballcap and chunky, black-rimmed glasses, he first approached a woman perched on a stool a ways down the bar. On the pretense of a surprise party that he was helping a friend set up, he asked his would-be accomplice to tell the fellow at the end of the bar that his wife urgently needed him at home. This version of Morley had known about his untimely demise for eight months by now and would surely see the message as a warning from his future self.

Unfortunately, when the helpful woman approached Morley at the bar, she abruptly veered away at the last moment, heading instead to the washrooms, having forgotten all about her mission.

He tried several more times with different customers, but the outcome was always the same. Just as they were about to deliver the message, it was as if they were emerging from a trance and momentarily didn't know where they were.

Undeterred, Morley tried another approach. In a different

disguise, he showed up a few minutes before his future self was due to arrive at the pub and gave Syd herself specific instructions to pass his regrets on to Morley that he couldn't meet as planned. He even went as far as writing down a fake name on a napkin for her—*Chris*—convinced that a physical message would make things stick. Syd had happily agreed, and, when her back was turned, Morley hustled into a dark booth in the corner to watch the result.

Sadly, before future Morley even arrived at the pub, Syd looked at the name on the napkin and shrugged confusedly before throwing it away.

It was hopeless. No matter what story Morley concocted or who he enlisted to help, the message never reached its intended recipient. His fate was set. And if he couldn't save himself, how could he ever save Collette?

On return to his present, Morley tossed his glasses and ballcap on the coffee table and slumped back on the couch. "Well, I guess that's that."

His eyes drifted over to his dining room table, where Syd had laid out his favorite meal two nights ago. He sighed, wishing she was sitting next to him now, comforting him like she had in his dream.

"This can't be it for me," he said to the empty apartment, the silence underscoring the lonely life he'd chosen. He couldn't stay there a minute longer.

Chapter Fifteen

Lost in a haze of dark thoughts, Morley barely registered the drive to his cabin. Once there, the normally invigorating scents of pine and cedar and the hushed whisper of wind through leaves offered no peace. Instead, they only served to remind him of how little time he had left to appreciate them.

Still hurting from his drinking binge the previous night, he poured himself a glass of sparkling water and settled into a chair on the deck. With his gaze fixed on the tree line across the lake, the stark beauty of it felt almost cruel now. Eight months. Just eight more months of sunsets, of cool breezes, of sweet, sweet life itself.

He pulled his phone out of his pocket meaning to record another note in his audio journal, but instead, he brought up all the entries that had anything to do with timeblinking and deleted every one of them.

"I will not burden anyone else with the knowledge of this power."

But as soon as the thought struck him, another one took its place. If he couldn't change his fate or Collette's, perhaps he could at least make these final months count for something. The talisman around his neck suddenly felt heavy with promise. He could pass it on, give someone else the extraordinary gift of timeblinking—and with it, a stern warning never to travel to the future.

His thoughts turned to the young patients he'd lost over the years. What if he was meant to offer a grieving couple the chance to see their little one again, to revisit their child in a healthier state in the past? He sat up straighter, convinced it was the entire reason he'd stumbled on the talisman's power. The question was: How would he choose who to give it to?

Just as the possibility began to take shape in his mind, a cruel reality dawned on him.

While the parents would be granted the power of seeing their son or daughter again, they would not be able to interact with the child in any way. It would be a torture worse than the grief they'd already endured.

Defeated, he got up and walked to the railing. "What good is the power?"

He unclasped the talisman from around his neck and studied it in his palm as if for the first time. It looked evil to him now. Cursed. He knew what he must do: dispose of it and never tell another living soul of its existence.

Then he remembered that, at some point, he would be passing the wretched thing onto Syd. His heart stuttered. It seemed that without even touching her, he'd condemned her to a terrible fate anyway. He moaned bitterly, his voice carrying on the wind like a wounded animal.

Peering out at the lake, he wondered what would happen if he simply threw the necklace as far and deep as he could into the water. With it languishing in the weeds at the lake's bottom, he would be saving Syd, and possibly others, from enduring the same pain. Moving toward the stairs leading down to the lake, he paused at the top step. "What if throwing it away changes Syd's life for the worse?"

As he wrestled with indecision, a new thought swooped in: Syd's identical twin, Isla, who had vanished when the girls were eleven years old. What if…what if the talisman was meant to help Syd uncover the truth behind Isla's disappearance all those years ago?

The more he thought about it, the more certain he became of the talisman's true purpose. Syd could go back to the moment she'd left her sister alone at the park and see for herself what had become of Isla.

"Yes!" he cried, coming to realize exactly how Syd had ended up with Collette's talisman. In fact, she'd even said it would happen in September, and now he knew the most likely date: September 13, during his usual visit to The Merryport Pub. The day a speeding truck would end his life.

Giving Syd the talisman would be his final act of kindness, a parting gift to the person he knew would benefit from it the most. But he would warn her to practice discretion. The power was seductive—he'd learned that much from his own obsession with it—and, if handled carelessly, it had the potential to ruin a life. He hoped Syd would recognize the dangers and limit herself to finding out what happened to Isla all those years ago, though he already knew that wouldn't be the case. Syd mentioned that she'd be using it to drop in on him soon, and he found himself looking forward to her visit.

As for his own plans with the talisman before parting with it in September, he resolved to timeblink only twice more. First, he would go back to his childhood and spend an entire day with his family. Or maybe a week. It seemed that no matter how long he remained in the alternate timeline, he would invariably be gone for four minutes and forty-four seconds in his present. And then he would go to France. There, he would follow Collette and himself around to all the places they explored on their fifth wedding anniversary, when they'd been at their happiest.

He would bask in the company of his special people one

final time, storing up memories like precious stones to carry him through his final months. And he would do it today.

Chapter Sixteen

On his return from his bittersweet journeys back in time, Morley sat pleasantly exhausted on his deck. He'd seen his mother helping young Morley with his math homework. He'd tagged along for a father-son fishing trip and got to enjoy his father's boisterous laugh when little Morley told a joke that was in no way funny. And then there was Collette—her golden eyes sparkling in the sunshine, her lean hand nestled in his as they strolled the narrow, winding streets of old Nice.

Now, gazing at the placid lake with those happy moments still fresh in his mind, the solitude didn't sting as much. He'd reveled in the fondest memories of his life, both in his childhood and as an adult, and he was eager to get on with living his remaining months to the fullest.

With a contented heart, he packed up his belongings and secured the cabin, resolving to go on a trip before September. A big one. And not a timeblink trip…a bona fide tropical or European vacation, which he hadn't done in years. He'd earned it. Maybe he would take a six-month sabbatical and explore the world. Why not? Who else would spend his fortune when he was gone?

"Look out, 2019, it's Morley Scott's year to travel!" he

said, firing up his Range Rover and starting down the tree-lined driveway. But his excitement quickly dissolved when his eyes locked on something that shouldn't be there. The black sedan.

Morley's jaw clenched. This was becoming more than just an annoyance—it was a threat to his privacy and potentially his safety. Enough was enough.

Once again entertaining the idea of calling the police, a better plan came to mind as he coasted toward the car idling at the curb. He would use the rugged terrain around his property to his advantage.

When he reached the road, instead of turning right toward the highway to town, he went left. He was betting his stalker would follow him up a decommissioned logging road that eventually looped back to the main highway.

As he'd hoped, the sedan followed.

"Ha! Who's in the driver's seat now?" Morley said as he pressed down on the accelerator, his powerful vehicle easily outpacing the sedan on the steep, pothole-riddled incline. Soon, the black car was absent in his rearview mirror.

Morley relaxed his grip on the steering wheel. "Not today, sir. Not today."

His victory, however, was short-lived. As he rounded a bend near the top of the hill three minutes later, he found the road blocked by massive concrete barriers, a "ROAD CLOSED" sign swinging lazily in the breeze.

"Great," Morley grumbled, hitting the brakes. "That would've been helpful to know at the bottom."

The truth was, there had probably been a notification in his mailbox at some point, but he didn't often read the community newsletters, preferring to use them as fire starters instead.

He glanced nervously in his rearview mirror—still no sign of the sedan. Maybe the jerk realized his car was no match for the treacherous road and had turned back. Morley would need to do the same.

He began maneuvering the SUV around in the narrow space. On one side, a sheer drop-off plummeted into a forested ravine with the swollen Deerleg Creek at the bottom. On the other, dense underbrush pressed against the gravel road. The SUV's tires barely found their grip on loose stones as Morley inched backwards, then forwards, working to position himself for the journey down the hill.

Just as he'd managed to get the vehicle turned around, the black sedan came hurtling around the bend, skidding to a stop a few feet from Morley's front bumper, effectively blocking his exit.

Morley's hands tightened on the wheel, his leather gloves softly squeaking as he watched the sedan's door swing open. A portly man with thick-rimmed glasses and an unkempt beard heaved himself out of the driver's seat and started toward him. As he drew closer, features that had been obscured by distance suddenly snapped into sickening clarity. Morley's mouth fell open in shock.

It was Dr. Freson.

But not the Freson he remembered from his unexpected trip to San Francisco a few days ago. This Freson was much heavier, his hair more gray than black, his once-angular features blurred by age and extra weight. Yet there was no mistaking those menacing eyes, now fixed on Morley with an intensity that made him shiver.

"Dr. Scott," Freson said, his voice muted through Morley's closed windows. "It's time we had a long-overdue conversation."

Morley sat frozen in his seat. What did Freson want *now*, eleven years after their meeting?

"Your necklace," the physicist said, his voice a blend of frustration and barely contained excitement. "I know you've been using it to traverse timelines."

Morley cut his engine and slid out of his vehicle, straightening to his full height. He had a good four inches on Freson and hoped his stature would intimidate the annoying man.

Morley crossed his arms. "I don't know what you're talking about."

"Time travel is what I'm talking about, my friend. And there's no point in denying it."

Morley forced a laugh, hoping it didn't sound as hollow as it felt. "Time travel? Wow. I think somebody's been sniffing too many chemicals in his lab."

Freson's puffy eyes narrowed. "Don't play dumb with me, Scott. Security found a pile of cash and your thrift-store loafers in the Berkeley library where you'd been sitting. Care to explain that?"

"I found better shoes."

"Don't mess with me, Scott. You've discovered temporal displacement, and you're going to explain to me how you do it."

"As I told you back in 2008, you were right. It was a prank Collette cooked up to finally get you back for tampering with her computer," Morley said, adding, "She always said your jealousy drove you to such a heinous act of vandalism that took her days to fix."

"That's how you're explaining it?" Freson scoffed. "Then tell me about the security footage. You disappeared into thin air, Scott. The security techs wrote it off as a glitch in the system, but I knew better."

Morley remained silent, his mind working overtime to come up with a plausible defense. He would not let this awful person bully him. He would not reveal his secret.

Freson's next words tumbled out in a rush. "After you visited my office asking questions about time manipulation and then subsequently disappeared, I couldn't brush it off as —as you put it—a prank. You yourself pointed out the age difference. You were older when I saw you at Berkeley in '08. And you look the same age now."

Morley shrugged. "Good genes."

Freson's face reddened. "Cut the bullshit! I've got you. I knew it the moment I saw the security footage in the library."

"If that's the case," Morley countered, "why didn't you contact me after that? Or Collette, for that matter?"

A wry smile formed on Freson's lips. "Because if you had truly time traveled, neither you nor Collette would have had any knowledge of it in 2008. You told me you'd stumbled on the power on January 14, 2019. I've waited eleven years for this meeting. And here we are."

"Man, I wish Collette was alive to see her prank come to fruition. Eleven years! That must be a record, hey? You're just going to have to accept the fact that you've been duped, Freson. Plain and simple."

The scientist's eyes shone with contempt. "Ah, but I have proof. You want to know how?"

"You're seriously delusional," Morley said, turning to get into his vehicle.

Freson lumbered in front of him, resting his back on the door. "Not half an hour ago, I watched you vanish from your deck and reappear five minutes later. Not once, but *twice*."

Morley gently nudged the physicist to the side and opened his door. "I'll set up an appointment for you with one of my friends in the psychiatric department."

Freson stepped in front of him again, bumping the door shut with his butt. "And I recorded it on my phone."

Morley's stomach dropped.

"The necklace," Freson said, his eyes drifting down to Morley's chest, where the dragonfly pendant lay hidden beneath his shirt. He brought his gaze back up and locked eyes with Morley. "You always hold it in your fingers right before you vanish."

A nervous laugh escaped Morley's lips before he could

stop it. "Dr. Freson, I sincerely hope you haven't shared these deranged beliefs with anyone else. You'd be the laughing stock of the scientific community."

Freson's face contorted with anger. "Of course I haven't told anyone, you idiot. Not until I can demonstrate the power for myself."

Morley shook his head, maintaining his denial amidst his jumbled nerves. "This is absurd. Kindly get your car out of my way. I'd like to go home."

"I'll move when you've told me how you do it."

"Are you sure that's how you want this to go?"

Freson glanced at his sedan blocking the road and returned with a smug smile. "You have no choice."

Morley had had enough of the man. He would use his SUV's brute force to drive around the parked car. A few scrapes and dents to his luxury vehicle hardly mattered anymore. But as he turned and reached for his handle, Freson's thick hand locked on his bicep and spun him around. The scientist's flushed face was inches from his own, his eyes wild. "Give me the necklace!" he yelled, spittle hitting Morley's cheek.

Instinct took over. Morley shoved the scientist, sending him stumbling backwards onto the hood of the sedan. But Freson recovered quickly, lunging at Morley with surprising speed.

Morley got Freson in a headlock and slammed him into the Range Rover's back quarter panel. Morley winced at the dull thumping sound his opponent's body made against the metal. Freson pushed back, driven by a maniacal determination, grabbing Morley around the waist. They both stumbled. Morley fell backwards onto the loose gravel, the impact knocking the wind out of him.

As Morley gasped for breath, the man scrabbled at Morley's neck, trying to get his hands on the talisman. Morley grabbed Freson's wrists, twisting them away, but he was unexpectedly strong in his frenzy and wrenched them out of Morley's grasp, resuming his quest for the talisman.

It was do or die. Still in a defensive posture on his back, Morley lifted his right leg and slammed his knee into Freson's nuts. Freson yelped and rolled away, curling into a tight ball. Morley scrambled to his feet and dashed to his vehicle. Just as he reached for the handle, he felt Freson jump on his back, clinging to him, his fingers plunging into the neckline of Morley's shirt. In Morley's battle to shake him off, they careened across the road and into the scrubby ditch.

They tussled for what seemed to Morley like several minutes but was likely only a few seconds as he repeatedly pushed Freson's hand away from his neck. Just when it seemed Freson was giving up, to Morley's horror, he saw the chain of the necklace stretched taut between them, the dragonfly dangling helplessly between them in the dim light of dusk.

With a last burst of energy, Morley lunged to a standing position, desperate to reclaim the talisman, but Freson jerked backward, his eyes wild with triumph. The chain broke with a soft snap and flew into the weeds in the ditch.

Both men dove for it, their shoulders colliding, sending them tumbling apart. Morley scrambled on his hands and knees to where he saw the talisman fall, and by some small miracle, he got his hands on both the chain and talisman and dropped them into his pocket before Freson came at him again.

The struggle resumed.

In their exhaustion, they staggered backwards, past the vehicles to the other side of the road. Morley was acutely aware of the embankment looming dangerously close as they scuffled, loose earth skittering over the edge with each faltering step.

Morley had to end this quickly before their fight culminated in tragedy. But Freson showed no signs of giving up. He was hell-bent to get his hands on the talisman.

Just as Morley feared they would tumble over the edge and into the ravine below, Freson broke away, his chest heaving. His hand disappeared behind his back and emerged a moment later with a glint of dark metal. Morley's heart leapt as Freson leveled a handgun at his chest.

"Enough," Freson panted, his hand trembling. "Give me the necklace, or I'll—"

Morley didn't let him finish. With a sudden lunge, he threw himself at Freson's middle, gambling everything on the element of surprise.

As the two men connected, Freson's foot skidded across the gravel, sending him off balance. He skittered backward, the cliff's edge surprising him. Loose stones shifted treacherously under his feet as he fought to stay upright.

Morley regained his footing and lunged forward, grabbing at Freson's windmilling hands, catching only air.

Freson's eyes caught Morley's in a final, terrified glance before he pitched off the embankment.

Morley covered his eyes, peeking through his fingers, powerless to look away from the horror unfolding below. Blood-chilling screams echoed in Morley's ears as the man's body bounced like a ragdoll off rocks and roots before coming to a sickening stop against a knee-high boulder near the bottom. It was a grim mercy. Without the rock to stop him, Freson would have plunged into the raging Deerleg Creek, where rushing waters were certain to sweep him downstream to the hundred-foot drop at Chapman Falls.

Morley flew into action, half-stumbling, half-sliding down the hilly terrain, his gloved hands grappling at branches and ferns to slow his descent.

When he reached the scientist, even all his years of medical experience couldn't have prepared him for the sight of the man's twisted, broken body. Freson lay on his back, his head resting at an unnatural angle against the boulder, his eyes wide with panic as his chest heaved and he struggled for air.

Morley kneeled, placing his hand on the physicist's shoulder. "Dr. Freson, can you hear me?" The response was a choked gasp.

In the dim evening light, Morley noticed a growing pool of blood under the man's head. "Hey, buddy," he said. "Help will be here soon."

Morley patted his pockets frantically, searching for his phone to call 911, realizing he'd left it in his vehicle.

"Hang on, friend. I'll be back lickety-split."

He started back up to the road, struggling for each foothold on the jagged, brush-choked terrain. His body felt as though he'd been hit by a bus after his tussle with Freson, and every muscle screamed as he ascended the steep grade.

Finally reaching the SUV, Morley yanked the door open and noted, to his dismay, that his phone wasn't in the dashboard mount like usual. He checked the center console, his duffle bag, and even under the seats. Nothing.

"Come on," he muttered, growing ever more anxious. Then it hit him—he'd left his phone on the deck at the cabin. "No, no, no," he groaned, slamming the door in frustration.

Knowing time was of the essence for his adversary, Morley turned and scrambled back down the embankment.

"I'm here," he said reassuringly, crouching beside Freson a few moments later. "I'm going to help you breathe, okay?"

But the scientist lay motionless, his eyes staring blankly up at the first stars of the evening. He was no longer moaning, and his labored gasping had ceased.

Freson was dead.

"Dr. Freson?" Morley said, jiggling the man's shoulder, hoping he was wrong. When there was no response, he removed his glove and pressed two fingers against the scientist's neck, searching for a pulse. None was to be found.

Morley sat back on his heels, devastated. The poor man had died a gruesome death. Alone.

He stared at Freson's lifeless form, calculating the ramifications of the scientist's tragic end. If anything, it proved what Morley had feared—that the promise of such power had the potential to turn the most rational person into a crazed lunatic.

A chilling vision of what could have been flooded his thoughts: Freson granting carte blanche power to the highest bidder. Morley imagined military applications, corporate exploitation, the potential chaos that would ensue once governments realized what they had. Perhaps Freson's death had prevented something far worse.

And yet…

Morley knew he couldn't protect this secret forever. Come September, the talisman would have a new guardian, someone who understood its immense responsibility. "You've entrusted me with this power for a reason," Syd had said that night over dinner, and though he hadn't fully understood the meaning of the words then, they resonated now. The power would be safe in her hands.

Morley took his gaze from the physicist's broken body to the top of the embankment, then back again. He knew what had to be done.

Moving on autopilot, Morley wrestled his glove back on and slipped his hand into Freson's wool coat pocket, finding what he was looking for instantly. He pulled out both Freson's phone and key fob and stood up, pocketing the key.

Assessing the phone, he couldn't believe a scientist of Freson's caliber would possess such an ancient device in this day and age, but there it was. A flip phone. The thing looked like a relic from the past, making Morley wonder if Freson himself had somehow time-traveled straight from the year 2000.

Giving quiet thanks for this fortuitous turn of events—an outdated, likely untraceable phone—Morley picked his way down to the creek and launched the device into the Deerleg's turbulent flow. He barely heard the sploosh as it entered the water.

He scurried back up to Freson's body and dropped to his knees, the enormity of it all hitting him full force.

"Oh God," he choked out, his hands shaking uncontrollably, his lips numb. "I never...I didn't mean..." He swallowed hard, struggling to think clearly. "You would have exposed everything, wouldn't you? Despite the consequences." His voice cracked. "Damn it, Freson. The world isn't ready for this kind of power—you just proved it."

He traced the outline of the pendant in his pocket. "And I've only got months left myself. My reputation, my life's work...it's all I have."

The lonely roar of the creek swallowed his words as he pushed himself off the ground.

"Please forgive me. But I have to take your death to my grave."

A few steps up the slope, Morley stopped. One last look to cement the surroundings in his mind. He would drop an anonymous tip to the police on September thirteenth if Freson's body hadn't already been found by then. "I'm so sorry. Rest in peace."

When Morley reached the road, he maneuvered Freson's car into the dense underbrush, hiding it from view. Then, limping, battered, and shaken, he returned to his own vehicle and climbed in.

Sitting for a few moments with his face buried in his hands, a small, serendipitous detail registered through his shock—his gloves. He pulled them away from his face and regarded them with wonder. They'd prevented him from leaving any fingerprints. He clung to this as a sign from the universe that he was doing the right thing.

The drive back to the city passed in a blur as Morley replayed the events over and over in his mind. He had killed a man. Accidentally, yes, but it had happened because of him. The horror of it pressed against his chest, even though he knew Freson's death might have prevented far worse consequences.

In his living room back at the condo, he stood at his window, catching his blurred reflection in the glass. Morley Scott, respected physician and accidental time traveler now carried a burden he never wanted—and a responsibility he couldn't ignore.

He reached into his pocket and withdrew the talisman, noting the damaged clasp where Freson had ripped it from his neck. The repair would be simple enough, certainly easier than living with what he'd done.

As his eyes roamed over the beguiling silver disc in his palm, he wondered if this was karma catching up with him. A life for a life. Or perhaps the price of playing with such an extraordinary power.

Whatever the reason, a fundamental truth crystallized in Morley's mind—one that would sustain him until his last breath at The Merryport Pub. While his fate had been chiseled in the bedrock of time, Syd's destiny remained gloriously unwritten.

Freson's Final Chapter

Learn what happened to Dr. Freson in this exclusive online news article from September 13, 2019…and check out Port Raven's biggest headlines of the day.

Scan this QR code to access the article:

Be there when Syd inherits the talisman and discovers its extraordinary power.

When Syd was eleven years old, her identical twin vanished from a park and was never found.

Now twenty years later, she's been given the power to go back to that day to uncover the truth once and for all. But what if the truth is too painful for Syd to face? What if she'd rather try to save Morley's life instead?

Read *TimeBlink*, Book 1 of the Syd Brixton series.

Acknowledgments

As Morley's story comes to an end, I'm grateful to the wonderful people who have helped breathe life into the Time-Blink universe.

To my amazing beta reading team—Jessica Cantwell, Ginny Martin, Alison Cairns, Patrick Zulinov, and Lee Gabel: your keen insights helped make this novella shine.

A special thanks to Dawn Dugle for her editorial prowess and for handing me an umbrella when the publication storm rolled in.

Heartfelt appreciation to my web design wizard, Alison Cairns, at Digital Rose Design Studio, and to Elizabeth Mackey, whose creative genius brings these book covers to life.

To my husband, Alistair, who continues to be my greatest supporter, ally, and occasional reality check. Thanks for your encouragement and for being my anchor in this big, crazy adventure.

And to every reader who has ever shared a shout-out about these books, whether online or in a conversation with a friend—I appreciate you. May your passion for adventure never wane and your shoes always make it to the other side!

About the Author

MJ Mumford's first novel, *TimeBlink,* debuted in 2020 amidst a worldwide health crisis. It wasn't the worst timing for a book launch. At a time when many of us were scared, anxious, or bored to tears, books provided the perfect escape to less precarious worlds.

As a huge fan of time-travel thrillers, suspense novels, and simmering love stories, MJ created The Syd Brixton Time-Blink Series to blend all three genres into one narrative.

When she's not dreaming up devious ways in which to torment her characters, MJ enjoys tap dancing, practicing yoga, and traveling to faraway places with her husband. Curiously, MJ never leaves home without her own trusty dragonfly talisman—an object rumored to be more than just decorative.

Hang out with MJ in the following places:
mjmumford.com

Also by MJ Mumford

TIMEBLINK

FLIGHT 444

DRAGONFLY